"Olivi

A sense of urgency gripped him. Calling her name, he rounded the corner into the escalator area.

A reflection in the glass diverted his attention. Pivoting, he realized the out-of-place shadow was a person, sprawled at the bottom of the steep escalators. Long black hair fanned across the shiny floor grate. A ribbon of dark liquid glistened beneath her cheek.

Olivia.

She wasn't moving.

Brady forced his leaden feet into motion. At her side, he fell to his knees and felt for a pulse. The breath whooshed from his lungs. Not dead.

"Olivia, can you hear me?" He searched for the blood source and discovered a deep gash behind her right ear.

She reacted to his probing fingers with an agonized moan.

"It's me. Brady. I'm here to help."

Her forehead pinched. When she attempted to sit up, she hissed and cradled her arm against her chest.

Brady reached out but didn't touch her. "What happened?"

Glancing at the floor above, she grimaced. "Someone pushed me."

Karen Kirst was born and raised in east Tennessee near the Great Smoky Mountains. She's a lifelong lover of books, but it wasn't until after college that she had the grand idea to write one herself. Now she divides her time between being a wife, homeschooling mom and romance writer. Her favorite pastimes are reading, visiting tearooms and watching romantic comedies.

Books by Karen Kirst

Love Inspired Suspense

Love Inspired Historical

Smoky Mountain Matches

Visit the Author Profile page at Harlequin.com for more titles.

DANGER IN THE DEEP

KAREN KIRST

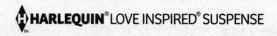
HARLEQUIN® LOVE INSPIRED® SUSPENSE

Recycling programs
for this product may
not exist in your area.

LOVE INSPIRED BOOKS

ISBN-13: 978-1-335-40258-5

Danger in the Deep

Copyright © 2020 by Karen Vyskocil

www.Harlequin.com

Printed in U.S.A.

My brethren, count it all joy when ye fall into divers temptations; Knowing this, that the trying of your faith worketh patience. But let patience have her perfect work, that ye may be perfect and entire, wanting nothing.

–James 1:2-4

Acknowledgments

Rachel Richardson, Sleep in the Deep educator–Rachel, I'm sure you weren't expecting me to actually follow through with my idea! I appreciate the time you took to answer my questions throughout this lengthy process. Your knowledge was invaluable in creating my heroine, as well as grasping aquarium operations.

J.T. Young–I appreciate your insight into what it means to be a USMC helicopter pilot. Thank you for patiently answering my many questions.

Andrew Benson–Thank you for sharing your diving knowledge and helping me craft plausible situations suited to an aquarium.

Jeff Sardella–Thank you for providing a clear understanding of light aircraft procedures and helping me with those all-important details.

Dan Rowe–You may not remember our chat last year, but I still have the notes. Thanks for telling me about your experiences as a USMC pilot.

Any mistakes are my own.

ONE

Olivia Smith entered the North Carolina Coastal Aquarium's vast ocean tank and slowly maneuvered through the balmy water. Something felt off about this dive. Her wet suit was uncomfortable. Her air cylinder was heavier than usual. She was having trouble adjusting to the rush of compressed gas and—for a terrifying moment—experienced a suffocating sensation. Bubbles spurted past her eyes, and the gurgling sound that accompanied being underwater pulsed in her ears.

Focus. There's no reason to panic. No one has drowned in this tank, and you're not about to be the first.

She concentrated on regulating her breathing and calming her agitated mind. This had nothing to do with her scuba gear and everything to do with the unpleasant night ahead—playing tour guide for a man who could barely tolerate her.

US Marine Corps pilot Captain Brady Johnson was her late husband's best friend, and he was on his way to her aquarium. More specifically, he was coming for tonight's Sleep with the Sharks overnight program. Olivia would be stuck with him the entire night as she guided his group of at-risk youth on an after-hours behind-the-scenes tour.

While Derek was alive, she and Brady had played nice. Well, *she* hadn't been playing. She genuinely liked Brady, and it hurt that he didn't feel the same. Now that Derek was gone, she didn't know how to act around the stand-offish pilot.

Their one and only green sea turtle, Terry, swam over to greet her. He was an aquarium favorite. He had survived a collision with a boat propeller and had lost one of his back legs, yet he'd retained his innate curiosity. He noticed her co-diver, Erin, and swam over to say hello. Beneath them, three sand tiger sharks glided in procession past one of the viewing areas.

A large cownose ray brushed her shoulder, reminding her to stay focused on the task at hand. While the myriad creatures in this tank were fed on a regular schedule and posed little threat, she had to keep her wits about her. Olivia signaled to Erin that she was descending to the deepest part of the tank. She was hoping to collect Atlantic spadefish eggs that she and her coworker Roman needed for their groundbreaking breeding program. If they could continue to successfully breed saltwater fish in the aquarium—an extremely challenging task—their need to catch wild populations would lessen. Other aquariums could utilize their findings and implement their own programs. The impact would be far-reaching and beneficial for all involved.

Her downward journey through the crystal-clear water took her between towering, misshapen artificial reef formations. At forty feet, their tank was one of the deepest in the country. Because some of the spaces were tight, Erin had chosen not to accompany her. Erin was notoriously claustrophobic and preferred to remain in the open water closer to the surface and interact with the sea creatures there.

Olivia reached the bottom and waved to the guests at the viewing window. A young girl decked out in neon pink caught her eye. The girl appeared to be transfixed by Olivia. She stood with her hands pressed to the glass, her eyes as big as quarters.

Charmed, Olivia swam closer and initiated a game of rock, paper, scissors. At first the girl's shyness got the better of her. Then, with her mother's encouragement, she played along. A crowd gathered. Olivia was enjoying herself until she lifted her gaze and recognized the blond man standing apart from the rest.

Why had he come early? The program didn't begin until after normal business hours.

Brady offered her a strained smile and half-hearted wave.

An emotional whirlpool churned up familiar frustration. Would it kill him to at least *act* happy to see her?

He'd checked on her three times in the eleven months since Derek's aneurysm. The visits had been brief and underscored with tension. Brady was no actor. His true feelings weren't hard to decipher. He didn't want to see her. He'd come because he owed it to his best friend. When he wasn't around, she convinced herself she didn't care what he thought. But then she'd see him again, and old wounds festered.

Lost in the past, she wasn't prepared when her mouth regulator erupted and spewed out her scuba cylinder contents. A torrent of bubbles invaded her mouth and hindered her vision. A smothering sensation stole over her as hundreds of thousands of gallons pressed in on her. The surface, far overhead, wasn't visible, and neither was her buddy, Erin.

Concentrate, Olivia. What's the solution?

She struggled to remember her instructor's advice. What had he said to do in this situation?

Of course. Breathe out the side, letting most of the bubbles escape. Sucking in multiple uneven breaths, she checked the pressure gauge. *Almost empty.* No, that couldn't be right. She'd made sure it was full during her predive check. It couldn't have released that much gas in the span of a minute or two.

She unhooked her small bailout bottle and put its accompanying regulator in her mouth. But nothing happened. She tapped the pressure gauge again and again. Why wasn't it working?

Dizziness overtook her.

She didn't have enough air to do a controlled ascent. Her time in the water wasn't an issue, but this depth was a major problem. Excess nitrogen in her bloodstream and tissues could form into bubbles if she rushed to the surface. Decompression sickness wasn't something she wanted to risk. Excruciating joint pain or skin rashes she could handle. But if those bubbles burst in her nervous system, she was facing paralysis or even death.

Glancing above her, she saw only a twisted maze of dense rock. Her vision blurred, and her lungs felt like twin balloons about to burst.

Olivia did what she'd been taught *not* to do.

She panicked.

Brady shouldered his way through the onlookers.

"Mommy, what's wrong with the lady?"

"I'm sure she'll be fine, sweetie." The young mother took her daughter's hand. "Let's go find a snack."

Brady took advantage of the vacated spot, which gave him a clearer view of this section of the tank. Unease built as Olivia swatted at the bubbles and shoved off the tank floor, heedless of her surroundings. When she almost rammed into the rock behind her, concerned murmurs rippled through the crowd around him.

Her long black hair floated around her face, further

hampering her vision. The bubbles continued to gush from her breathing device. She was in danger of running out of air if she didn't act soon. And if she continued to panic, she could hit her head against the rock formations and lose consciousness.

The intensity of the apprehension welling up inside surprised him. Every single critical thought he'd entertained about Olivia Smith evaporated as he watched her struggle. Whatever her motives for marrying Derek had been, she'd made him happy during the short time they were together.

Brady went in search of an aquarium employee. He found a teenage boy at a drinks station.

"There's an emergency in the shark tank. A diver is in trouble."

The boy stared at him in confusion.

"Do you have a comms system?" Brady demanded.

"Sir?"

Assuming his sternest stare, he grated out, "Take me to the tank entrance."

"But you're not allowed—"

"I'm a friend of Olivia Smith's." That was a stretch, but a necessary one. "She needs assistance. Now."

His Adam's apple bobbing, he abandoned the queue of customers and jogged up the ramp. "This way."

As they dodged curious guests, Brady found himself praying for the woman he'd spent months mentally maligning. *Olivia's in trouble, Lord. Please help her. For Derek's sake.*

They entered an employee-only stairwell and raced to the top level. Bursting into a room containing large plastic tubs stocked with tiny fish and glass jars hooked to tubes, the boy led him through a second door that opened onto a walkway surrounding the enormous tank.

A short, curly-haired man standing at a dry-erase board printed with feeding schedules frowned at them.

"Leon, why did you abandon your post?" He studied Brady. "This area is restricted, sir. You'll have to return to the guest viewing area."

Brady bent over the railing and searched in vain for a glimpse of her. "Olivia's down there with malfunctioning equipment. She's running out of air."

Below the rippling surface, schools of fish swam in formation, oblivious to the disturbance at the bottom.

The sky was Brady's domain, not the water. But he'd brave the deep blue if it meant saving Derek's widow. He headed to the dive dock. The other man was retrieving a wet suit, but he wasn't moving fast enough. Didn't he realize every second mattered?

Spotting a second diver, Brady made a split-second decision. He shucked off his jacket and placed his cell in the folds. Then he jumped in and, ignoring the shouts of protest behind him, sliced through the water to her side. The other diver was near the surface, but on the far side of the tank. It seemed to take forever to reach her. Behind the mask, her eyes went wide.

He grabbed her arm and gestured to the bottom. At first, she didn't respond. Frustrated, Brady started to tow her along with him. Finally, she seemed to understand, because she wrestled free, gestured for him to return to the dock and then darted toward the reef formations.

Straining for air, he returned to the surface and a flurry of activity.

"Come out of there at once!" The curly-headed man looked as if he'd like to feed Brady to the sharks, while Leon's expression was frozen in horror.

The realization of what he'd done registered. He was in a tank with multiple creatures that might decide he'd make a tasty snack. They were used to the aquarium staff sharing their habitat, but a random guy who had scant knowledge about their feeding preferences or behaviors? Focusing on the dock, he wasted no time getting there.

Water sluiced down his body onto the metal grid beneath his sodden tennis shoes. While the older man read him the riot act, he scanned the water for Olivia.

Would the other diver reach her in time?

"Good, security's here. You're going to be escorted off the premises, sir."

Movement beside him belatedly registered, and he looked up into the grim visage of the security guard.

"You'll need to come with me, Mr.—"

"It's Captain Johnson. Look, I know I broke a rule of some sort, and I apologize. I will leave without a fuss, but first I need to see that Olivia is all right."

The guard's nostrils flared, and he rested his hand on the weapon at his hip. "You will leave now."

Brady hadn't ever been arrested or spent a night in jail. The prospect hadn't even occurred to him. Now he found himself debating the cost of his actions. He wasn't leaving until Olivia was out of that tank.

"I see them!" Leon shouted.

Brady spotted the two divers. The brunette was assisting Olivia through the water and sharing her air with her. The fact she was conscious was a good sign, but he couldn't give in to relief just yet.

A hand clamped on to his shoulder. "Let's go."

"Can't he stay a little longer?" Leon piped up. "He's friends with Olivia."

The man in charge—James, according to his name badge—eyed Brady with skepticism. "How do you know her?"

"She was married to a pilot friend of mine." A trivial label for the friendship that had saved his career, and possibly even his life. Grief, that terrible companion that caught him unawares and threatened hard-won control, slammed into him again.

"You knew Derek?"

He cleared his throat. "We met in flight school."

James nodded to the guard, who retreated to the railing with a disgusted scowl. The group returned their attention to the divers, who appeared to stop every few feet and tread water. When the pair finally reached the dock, he put a hand beneath Olivia's arm and helped her out of the water.

"Brady." Once on her feet, she shifted out of his grip, removed her eye mask and peeled the wet strands off her face. He noticed her hands were trembling. "How did you get up here?"

"Leon brought me. Are you all right?"

"I'm fine." Her rich brown eyes told another tale. The incident had shaken her. Her nose crinkled. "Why are you wet?"

Leon grinned. "He jumped in to help you."

Her jaw sagged. "You did what?"

Olivia's disbelief was to be expected. He'd frozen her out, not taking pains to hide his suspicions that she was using Derek to perpetuate a fantasy. He'd seen it all too often…local girls who painted pilots in a glamorous light and thought they could achieve a Top Gun dream life. She'd had Derek talking marriage after a week. That wasn't a sign of an authentic bond. It was the sign of a campaign launched to dazzle and distract.

"What happened down there?"

"Regulator free-flow." Seeing his lifted brows, she amended, "The gas started discharging from my cylinder. My regulator malfunctioned."

James turned to her. "Didn't they teach you how to handle that in dive school?"

"They did." Olivia's black brows pulled together. "It hasn't happened to me before, and I lost my cool. I'm sorry for worrying the guests." Tugging off her fingerless gloves, she looked at Brady. "Did I frighten the little girl?"

"Her mother distracted her."

"What about your backup?" James persisted.

Brady bristled at his accusatory tone, but he muzzled the brewing retort. This man could be Olivia's superior, and he didn't want to get her in trouble.

Sinking onto a metal bench, she tugged off her fins one by one. "Something's wrong with it. My primary cylinder, too. I checked both before I went in, and they were fine."

The brunette interjected. "She's right. We inspected our equipment at the same time."

"The gauges showed they were full," she said, straightening. "Down there, it was a different story. My large cylinder was nearly empty and the pony bottle was completely out."

James planted his hands on his hips. "It would be unusual for one to malfunction, but not both."

Silence reigned. Brady voiced what no one else seemed willing to. "Did you leave your equipment unsupervised between the time of your inspection and the time you entered the water?"

Olivia let her fins clatter to the floor. "What are you suggesting?"

"Is it possible that someone wanted to sabotage your dive?"

TWO

Sabotage? The word wasn't part of her everyday life. Olivia understood why a military man like Brady would consider it. He was conditioned to combat evil in the world.

"There isn't a single person on the aquarium payroll whom I'd consider capable of such an act."

He held her gaze. "Capable in knowledge or intent?"

"There are plenty of certified divers here, but no one who'd willingly damage scuba equipment."

"Not even for a joke?" Brady said.

"That's not my idea of a joke."

Erin sat beside her. "You were called away for an urgent phone call, remember?"

Olivia had forgotten about the summons. She'd been told that an American Zoo Association representative was requesting information about the upcoming fund-raiser, but when she'd gotten to the phone, the line was dead. She dismissed any thoughts of foul play. This was her second home. Her coworkers were her substitute family. The aquarium had kept her in the Jacksonville area after Derek's death. If she didn't adore her job, she would've returned to Cherokee in the western part of the state or even sought employment at a different aquarium.

"True," she said, "but you were here."

Worry lines dug into Erin's forehead. "Actually, I dashed to the restroom."

Brady bent and retrieved his jacket. The long-sleeved

gray shirt he wore, wet from his foray into the tank, ad-hered to his muscular shoulders and biceps like glue. He straightened and regarded them with his arctic blue-gray gaze. His customary air of authority—gleaned from flight school and his subsequent climb through the ranks—was in place. He was accustomed to being respected and ad-mired, not befriended or loved. She believed he preferred it that way. Why else would he work so hard at keeping others at arm's length?

A shame, because he had a lot to offer. She'd wit-nessed his tireless commitment to community service. Each Christmas season, he was instrumental in local gift collection for Toys for Tots. He gave his time and energy each week to kids who lacked positive role models. She'd seen evidence of his compassion and selflessness, his pa-triotism and work ethic. She'd even seen him let go and have fun. He and Derek had played together on a church basketball team. On the court, he'd forgotten his child-hood wounds, forgotten the drive to prove his worth and simply enjoyed himself.

Olivia wanted to get to know *that* Brady, but she doubted she'd ever have the chance.

"So there was a window of opportunity?" he said, scat-tering her thoughts.

Standing to her feet, she unzipped the wet suit. "It was a fluke. A one-off."

James, who'd been looking over the equipment, joined them. "I'm inclined to agree. We'll have these serviced before using them again."

Brady pushed his damp hair off his forehead. "You aren't going to do an in-house investigation?"

"I'll discuss it with the director. For now, it's enough to know that Olivia is unharmed," James said. He gestured to the guard, who left his spot at the railing.

"It's time for you to go, Captain Johnson."

Olivia glanced between the men, realizing they intended to evict him from the aquarium. That meant he wouldn't be able to stay for the program. She considered seizing the chance to avoid spending time with Brady but quickly dismissed it. He'd entered the shark tank to try to help her.

"Let him stay."

Everyone stared at her.

"Please, James. He won't be jumping into any more tanks, I promise."

Relenting, James lectured Brady about safety protocols and sent the guard on his way.

"The kids get here in an hour. Olivia, may I speak to you alone before they arrive?"

She masked her reluctance with a nod. "I'll meet you in Stingray Bay."

When he'd left with Leon, Erin shot her a *confess-all* look. "Who is that?"

How to define their non-relationship? Someone she'd hoped could be a friend?

Regret pinched her heart. "He was important to my husband."

Brady didn't have to wait long. Olivia met him in the humid glass enclosure that housed an interactive stingray exhibit, lemurs and a butterfly garden. She'd changed into the standard uniform of khaki pants and a soft blue polo. Her fine black hair was woven into an intricate braid that accentuated her striking features. If Olivia was aware of her appeal, she didn't show it.

Shoving the unwanted appreciation aside, he thought of the secret Derek had entrusted him with months before his death. He still couldn't quite believe that the man he'd known for years had been using a fake identity. Sometimes, when Brady wondered if he'd dreamed the conversation, he dug out the newspaper clippings about the missing mafia heir and reread them.

He considered what Olivia's reaction to the news might be. Would she feel betrayed? Angry? Disillusioned? After all, her perfect pilot hadn't been what he'd presented himself to be.

Brady wouldn't tell her, of course. He couldn't bring himself to deliberately wound her.

He continued to observe the stingrays in their shallow touch tank. "Feeling any lingering effects from your ordeal?"

"A mild headache and hefty dose of embarrassment. Scaring the guests is not in my job description."

He could've told her that it wasn't her fault, but the words stuck in his throat. His conscience pinched him. Derek was gone. It no longer mattered what her ulterior motives for marrying him had been.

"What about you?" she said. "Sorry you took a swim in the shark tank?"

"No." He turned toward her. "I am glad I had an extra change of clothes in the car, however."

Sunlight rendered her hair an even glossier shade of jet and lent her complexion a satiny sheen. He wasn't supposed to notice these things. He locked his hands behind his back and put extra inches between them.

"What were you doing down there alone?"

"A colleague and I are working on an innovative project. I was down there to collect fish eggs."

"Is there anyone who'd benefit from its failure?"

"The aim of this project is to minimize our impact on the oceans' fish population. Successfully raising larval saltwater fish here will preclude the need to harvest them from the wild. I can't think of anyone who would stand in the way of that."

"Is there an employee who'd like to have your position? Someone who'd try and frighten you into quitting?"

"You're thinking like a marine, not a civilian."

"Military or no, evil exists in the world. You shouldn't dismiss the possibility the damage was intentional."

"Not in this case, Brady." She paused as an announcement came over the speakers. The aquarium was closing in half an hour. A family of four exited the area, leaving them alone. "What did you want to talk to me about?"

He had to force the next words from his mouth. "The anniversary of Derek's death is in a few weeks. Will you meet the deadline?"

Sadness stole over her, only to be shuttered seconds later. "I've already put a deposit on a new place. I'll be out in time."

As the widow of an active-duty marine, she'd been given a year to move out of base housing. She'd taken advantage of the grace period, using the months since Derek's death to take stock of her options. Brady drove past the air station housing area every morning on his way to squadron headquarters and every evening on his way home.

"Where?"

"A warehouse apartment near downtown. It's more compact, but it has a fantastic view of the river."

"I'll help you move." Derek would want him to help her, to see her settled in her new life.

"I'm considering hiring a moving company."

"That won't be cheap."

"I'll figure it out."

"Why don't you let me and some of the guys do it?" The entire squadron mourned Derek's loss, and any one of them would leap at the chance to help her. "You don't have family here."

"My coworkers stand in for them."

"Olivia—"

"Brady, stop the charade." Resignation tugged at her lips. "Derek's not here to applaud your performance."

"I don't know what—"

"For whatever reason, you've never given me a chance to win your respect or friendship."

The genuine hurt in her eyes knocked him back a step. Surely, she didn't care what he thought? That would indicate she wasn't the shallow groupie he'd painted her to be.

You're wrong about her, Derek had argued the one time they'd discussed Brady's reservations. *Time will prove you wrong.*

More and more, he was beginning to suspect he *had* made a mistake. Nothing supported his initial assessment of her character. In fact, her behavior suggested the opposite. She'd been a devoted, supportive wife during their brief, seven months' union. She'd been unfailingly kind to Brady, despite his refusal to trust her. She hadn't tried to sabotage his and Derek's friendship, either.

Have you considered that this wasn't about her? That you'd be suspicious of anyone who'd intruded on your oldest, closest friendship?

Cold flushed through him. If that was true, he'd been grossly unfair.

She lifted her chin in challenge. "Let's just get through this night, okay? And then we agree to steer clear of each other. No more pity visits. They don't benefit either of us."

Pity visits? Didn't she realize she was his last link to his best friend, and that no matter their history, he'd *needed* to see her?

Before he could think of a proper response, a young

woman emerged from a door beside the lemur exhibit and hailed Olivia with a hardy wave.

"Do you have time to get the snacks and drinks ready for tonight?"

"Maya. I thought Erin was working the program with me."

"I asked her to switch. I have plans tomorrow night." Her jaw sawing on bubblegum, she stuffed her hands into her back pockets and regarded him with wide eyes. "Hello."

"Brady, this is Maya Fentress."

Grinning, Maya blew a giant pink bubble. Taller and stockier than Olivia, she had chin-length brown hair streaked with pink and an eyebrow piercing. Freckles dusted her pert nose and rounded cheeks. She looked to be in her early twenties.

"Pleased to meet you, Maya."

"Are you one of the dads?" She glanced at his left hand, presumably looking for a ring.

"No, I don't have any kids."

Family life wasn't for him. He'd known it from a tender age and had accepted his lot. His own parents hadn't thought him worthy of attention or love. They'd discarded him as if he were secondhand goods, dumping him at his grandmother's house shortly before his tenth birthday. As his school counselor had said often enough, he had abandonment issues. A tidy label that didn't scratch the surface of what his childhood experiences had done to him.

THREE

The grief ravaging Brady's face siphoned the breath from her lungs. She lifted her hand to touch him, to impart comfort, only to catch herself. He didn't want anything from her.

"Not married, huh?" Speculation ripened Maya's eyes. She hadn't noticed his unease. Not surprising, considering Maya's chief concern was herself.

"Brady volunteers with a local program pairing volunteer mentors with at-risk youth," Olivia quickly interjected.

"Most of the kids in our group have never been to an aquarium before," he said, his voice rusty.

"It's our most popular event. Stick with me, and I'll make sure you have a blast." She giggled. "The kids, too."

"Maya, why don't you gather the snacks while I show Brady the auditorium?"

She opened her mouth to protest but, at Olivia's pointed stare, rubbed his arm instead. "I'll see you soon, Brady."

Olivia ushered him out of the stingray area. Riding the escalator to the first floor, she studied his stoic profile and found herself wishing he'd open up to her. Holding in that amount of grief and anger robbed the present of its joy. Derek had mentioned Brady had had a tough childhood, but he hadn't given many details. If only he were here... he'd had the ability to shred Brady's reserve.

"I should warn you that Maya can be a lot to handle."

He gave her a tight smile. "I gathered as much."

"How long have you volunteered with these kids?"

"Over five years."

Stepping off the escalator, they circumvented this building's main entrance and descended yet another escalator to where the group's event would originate. He opened the auditorium door for her.

"We'll start the program with an up close and personal experience with a couple of our favorite reptiles, and then we'll go to the feeding room, where we'll discuss what types of foods the animals eat. Pizza will be served before we tour the two buildings."

They reached the stage. "Is this a regular part of your job? Derek never mentioned it."

The casual mention of him was jarring. No one spoke his name anymore. Her sisters tiptoed around the subject. Her coworkers avoided it completely. As time marched on, Olivia found herself wanting to talk about him. Acting as if he hadn't existed—simply to spare her pain—wasn't fair to his memory.

"I subbed for someone a couple of months ago and enjoyed it." She motioned to the vacant room. "Being in the aquarium at night is a unique experience. It's peaceful."

His blond brows shot up. "In my experience, peace and kids don't go together."

"You'll see what I mean. Especially when they're in the shark tunnel, snug in their sleeping bags, and everyone drifts to sleep watching the fish swim overhead."

Commotion at the top left entrance shattered the hushed stillness. An aquarium employee ushered twenty middle and high school kids into the auditorium. Chatter and laughter bounced off the paneled walls as they dropped their backpacks and sleeping bags and thundered down the steps.

"How many hours until bedtime?" Brady drawled, rubbing his jaw.

His words were belied by the high fives he doled out. One of the younger boys, Michael, gave him a hug. The affection on Brady's face and the way he mussed the boy's hair spoke volumes. The unflappable Marine pilot who looked as if he could eat nails for breakfast had a marshmallow heart, at least when it came to these kids.

She wished things could be different. It would've been nice to bond with someone who cared about Derek as much as she did.

He introduced her to his fellow volunteers—Norman, who resembled a wise owl, and Dana, a frazzled middle-aged mom—before spouting off the names of everyone in the group. Olivia's previous reluctance faded. Maybe the night wouldn't be as onerous as she'd thought.

Maya arrived with the boa constrictor, drawing the boys and girls into a tight knot around her. Their curiosity remained evident as they progressed to the feeding room with walk-in freezers and coolers stocked with everything from vegetables to tiny shrimp. As she interacted with them, Olivia managed to forget her diving ordeal.

While they were wolfing down pizza and guzzling caffeinated sodas, she joined Brady at the windows. He twisted the cap off an orange juice bottle and offered it to her.

Shaking her head, she studied the tables' occupants. "Why them? Why not the homeless shelter or food bank?"

His eyes had a bleak look that saddened her.

"Growing up in my grandmother's home, I didn't have a positive male influence. My grandmother was a sweet soul, but her health was frail. No one bothered to step into my life and make a positive impact. I longed for that, even though I couldn't pinpoint the specific need at the time."

"How old were you when you went to live with her?"

His lips thinned. "Ten."

Olivia could imagine his confusion and disappointment. Then, to have to take on the role of caregiver at such a young age. Her heart hurt for the child he'd been.

Her parents hadn't had the best of relationships, but her mother had done everything in her power to create a loving, nurturing environment for Olivia and her siblings. She'd never doubted she was loved and wanted.

"You're doing for these kids what someone should've done for you. You're choosing to care."

His broad chest rose and hitched. Guzzling the juice, he tossed the empty glass in the recycle bin and pointed to the farthest table. "I'm going to talk to Michael and Cameron."

In the past, Olivia would've viewed his abrupt departure as a rejection. Now she saw his behavior for what it was—an attempt to avoid deep-rooted anguish. Maybe she truly wasn't his favorite person. Maybe he hadn't liked her and Derek together. But that wasn't the whole story. Captain Brady Johnson was a complex, mysterious man whom she would probably never truly know.

But she could pray for him. Why hadn't she thought to do that before?

I'm sorry, Lord, for fretting over this issue instead of bringing it to You. I don't know the details of his private pain, but You do. Please help him.

Olivia started gathering the empty pizza boxes and other trash. Maya popped over. "Are you and the hunky captain involved?"

"Brady served with my husband. We're acquaintances."

"Would you date him?"

She tied a thick garbage bag with more force than necessary. "No."

The Marine pilot possessed the aristocratic good looks and bearing of royalty. His flaxen hair, light eyes and fair skin was a memorable combination. He was tall and built of lean, ropy muscle. That didn't mean she was affected. Because of his connection with Derek, Brady was firmly in the off-limits zone. Besides, she was still in mourning.

"Good."

"Don't you have a boyfriend?"

"We're not serious."

Olivia clamped her lips together. Thanks to her recent love interest, Maya had started hanging around a rough crowd who skirted the law. She'd tried to warn the younger woman, but Maya hadn't been receptive. In fact, she'd been hostile. There was no use telling her that Brady rarely dated.

"I'm taking these out to the dumpsters."

Maya grunted a response. Olivia hauled the cumbersome bags through the employee kitchen and out an exit that emptied into a single, paved lane. The heavy door slammed shut with a bang, and she jerked. The thick hedges opposite twisted together like grotesque hands. She dragged the bags around the corner to the trash receptacles, which were located at the edge of an employee parking lot that linked the River Expedition to the Ocean Adventure building. Before tonight, she wouldn't have wondered what or who could be hiding in the shrubbery.

She shivered as a brisk wind flattened her pants against her legs and nipped at her hair. Goose bumps marched along her exposed forearms. Her coat would've come in handy, but as it was a consistent temperature inside the aquarium, she typically left it in her office during shifts.

Crossing the isolated lot, Olivia felt vulnerable. The handful of lampposts weren't enough to combat the complete November darkness. The panic she'd experienced in the shark tank threatened to erupt.

Ridiculous. She increased her pace. *Brady's suspicions are just that...groundless suspicions.*

At the dumpster, she yanked open the side slot and pushed in the bags. Somewhere in the night, a bottle dropped and rolled across concrete. Olivia yelped and pressed her hand to her thrumming heart.

"This has to stop," she said aloud, squinting into the shadows.

She would *not* let her imagination play tricks on her.

A rustling noise behind the dumpster had her backing up. When a calico cat leaped out and greeted her with a plaintive meow, she bent to pet it.

"You frightened me, you know that?" she crooned.

Crouched at its level, she spied an odd-shaped bag propped against the concrete-block barrier. The wind tangled with the top flaps and revealed what appeared to be a scuba cylinder.

Olivia reached out, pulled the plastic lower and tried to make sense of what she was seeing. Two cylinders. One silver regular size and a backup orange pony bottle.

Her cylinders. The jagged, superficial scratch near the bottom of the big one proved it.

Her mind whirled. Why were they out here? James couldn't have had time to get someone out to service them.

Brady's allegations threw her reasoning into a tailspin. Could he be right?

Could someone have wanted her to encounter trouble in the shark tank?

"Where did Olivia go?" Brady asked.

Annoyance sparked in Maya's eyes. "She took out the garbage." With both hands balanced on the child-size plastic chair in front of her, she leaned close. "Tell me more about flying. You pilot a Huey helicopter?"

"SuperCobra. Twin-engine attack helo." Brady gestured to the kitchen visible through an open doorway. "Did she use that exit?"

"Olivia's fine. Tell me more about flying."

"Maybe later." He strode past the long lunchroom-style tables.

"Captain, look!" Grinning, Michael lifted a slice of pizza stacked with chocolate chip cookies and took a bite.

He gave him a thumbs-up. "Fix me one of those."

Beaming, the boy nodded. "Yes, sir!"

In the kitchen, he heard a muffled pounding and hurried to open the door. Olivia stood on the stoop, shivering, deep grooves of worry carved into her brow.

"What's the matter?"

"Come with me." She seized his hand. "I need to show you something."

As she led him into the night, he couldn't help but notice how their palms fit together...and how cold her skin was. Shrugging out of his jacket, he insisted she put it on.

"Look." Pulling the lapels together, she directed his attention to a pair of diving cylinders. "These are the ones I use." She ran her fingertip over a scratch. "I knocked into metal lockers a month or so ago."

"We need to speak to James and find out why he'd discard them here."

"He's already gone for the day."

"Do you have his cell number?"

She tugged her braid free of the jacket collar. "In my office. I lock my phone in my desk drawer during working hours."

"I'll go with you to make the call."

"The tour—"

"The kids are preoccupied right now. They won't notice our absence."

After briefing Norman and the other adults, Olivia led him through the darkened, deserted aquarium. They traversed a maze of high walkways and stairs in a multistory area dominated with large tanks featuring river fish. A shallow pool of water occupied the floor level, and they had to cross on skinny platforms. He understood how she could think it peaceful without the hordes of visitors. Still, there was an almost eerie quality to it.

Voices greeted them as they neared the main entrance. A spindly gentleman in a black uniform mopped the floor as another man spun his car keys on his finger.

"Good evening, Mr. Ludwig." Olivia greeted the pair. "Roman, I thought you'd gone home already."

Roman stopped the keys' motion and, balling them into his palm, sized Brady up from behind rimless glasses. "My car won't start. I'm waiting on a friend to give me a ride home."

"I'm sorry to hear that. I hope it's an inexpensive fix."

"I do, too."

"This is Captain Johnson." Olivia gestured to Brady. "Roman and I are working together on the breeding program I told you about."

Brady initiated a handshake. He guessed Roman to be in his late thirties, early forties. He had wavy brown hair and a short, scruffy beard streaked with silver and reddish gold. Like Olivia, he wore khakis and a blue polo bearing the aquarium emblem.

"I heard about your dive," Roman said, his bushy brows descending over sharp gray eyes. "Any chance you got our eggs before you ran out of air?"

The guy's disregard for Olivia's welfare irked Brady.

"Sorry to disappoint you," she responded good-naturedly. "Why don't you get your dive cert and retrieve them yourself?"

"Touché." Through the floor-to-ceiling glass, a car pulled into view and honked. "That's my ride."

"See you tomorrow."

As they entered a bunker-like underground corridor linking the aquarium's river and ocean buildings, Olivia shot Brady a sideways glance. "Roman's grumpiness has earned him a nickname around here. We call him 'Gruffy' behind his back."

"Do you like working with him?" His voice echoed off the stark cement walls and floor.

"He's dependable. I can't recall a time he's come in late or called in sick."

"Would you say he's an equal contributor to your project?"

She fiddled with one of her silver dolphin earrings. "While he doesn't generate ideas, he's a decent problem solver."

The corridor was a dank, musty space that seemed to stretch on for miles. Emerging into the Ocean Adventure lobby, he breathed in fresh, warm air. They navigated the escalators—turned off for the night—and various exhibit areas before entering the office wing.

"This is James's." A slim glass window showed the room was empty. "Mine is farther down."

Located at a midway point, her box of an office was made smaller by shelves stuffed with trade books and magazines. Colorful works of art showcasing her Native American heritage were wedged into every available wall space. As she retrieved her phone and made the call to James, Brady studied a smooth, black pottery bowl with a carving of two feathers. He'd heard her talk about the

Qualla Arts and Crafts cooperative, located in Cherokee, and the fact her mother crafted baskets to sell there.

He noticed the change in her voice as she ended the call. "What is it?"

Sliding her phone into her pocket, she met his quizzical gaze and shrugged. "James said my cylinders are in his office. He spoke with the equipment company here in town, and a rep is supposed to come on Monday."

"Do you have a key to his office?"

"There's a master set in the meeting room."

When she'd retrieved the key, they entered and she flicked on the light.

"There are cylinders, all right." Brady pointed to the pair propped against the desk chair. "They look identical to the ones by the dumpster."

She performed a quick inspection. "Except there isn't a scratch."

"Walk me through what happened right before your dive."

"I changed into my wet suit. I joined Erin in the tank area, and we did a methodical check of our equipment. My cylinders were full. The regulator was free of salt buildup and debris." Sagging against the desk edge, she spread her hands. "I didn't notice anything out of the ordinary. At least not with my gear."

"Which somehow ended up in a garbage bag outside the other building. This building has its own trash area?"

"Yes, of course."

"You said you received a phone call right before the dive?"

"I was told a representative from AZA, the American Zoo Association, needed to speak to me about the upcoming gala. It's an important night for Roman and I, since we're presenting our findings. We're hopeful the success we've had until this point will net further support and other aquariums will follow suit."

"Who summoned you?"

"One of the secretarial staff. Sarah." She ran her palms over her pants. "When I got to a phone, there was no one on the line. I assumed they'd gotten impatient and would call back later. When I returned to the dive dock, Erin was suited up and waiting for me."

"She said she was in the restroom for a few minutes."

Olivia contemplated the cylinders as if they were bombs set to explode. "You think someone switched mine out for these defective ones."

"I do. The question is who and why? Are you and Erin on good terms?"

"Erin's a sweetheart. She wouldn't do this."

"Are there security cameras in the tank area?"

She popped up. "There are two."

Together, they headed to the security office, but it was locked. The one guard on duty overnight spent much of his time touring the premises.

"It'll have to wait until morning," she stated. "We've been gone long enough, as it is."

"This is important, Olivia."

"So is your kids' experience. I'm not going to waste another half hour or more tracking down the guard. It'll keep."

Brady stifled his complaints. Olivia was clearly having trouble accepting that her safe haven had been tainted. Until they could view those video feeds and get those discarded tanks to the police, he'd make a point to stay near her.

Weariness pulled Olivia closer to sleep, even as she continued to ponder her predicament. There could be no denying someone in her world wanted her to suffer. A devastating thought. In the months since Derek's death, the aquarium had become her refuge and the employees her support net.

Brady had remained within arm's reach of her the entire evening, as if he were her covert bodyguard. His closeness had increased her unease. At least the kids hadn't seemed to notice anything amiss. Their interactions with Brady revealed the depth of their respect and genuine admiration for him. And it was clear he cared about them, too. There was nothing forced or stiff about his demeanor when he engaged with them. It was a side she wished she could see more often.

Despite the HVAC system hum, laughter trickled down from the landing above. Everyone was supposed to be in their sleeping bags, not wandering through the building. Olivia pushed her blankets aside and, slipping on her shoes, left the cot she'd situated at the lower end of the tunnel. Lamplight outside the massive, floor-to-ceiling glass wall cast enough light for her to navigate the motionless escalator.

At the top, she discovered a high school couple in the penguin exhibit. The boy and girl weren't paying attention to the penguins. Hands entwined, they were whispering and laughing, their shy smiles evidence of their mutual crush.

Olivia cleared her throat, and they leaped apart.

"Time to return to the tunnel, you two," she said lightly.

"Yes, ma'am."

The girl's head bowed, she scurried away, the boy on her heels.

"Young love," she muttered, recalling the naivete of her teenage years.

Behind the glass, she watched a penguin glide beneath

the water and perform tricks. Olivia never lost her fascination for God's amazing creatures. His imagination and wisdom were limitless. She didn't know how much time passed before the penguin tired of his antics and returned to the rock ledge.

Her watch warned her there weren't many hours left to sleep. She abandoned the exhibit and skirted a thick blue support beam. A faint sound, like the scrape of a shoe against drywall, reached her. Her nape prickled. Whirling around, she searched the shadows and willed her heartbeat to slow. There weren't any boogeymen out to get her. Her tumultuous day was making her imagine the worst.

She walked at a fast clip toward the escalator. Olivia reached for the black cushioned handrest. Her fingers never grasped it.

A whisper of hot breath fanning over her nape was her only warning before two hands settled against her back and shoved.

Olivia's scream lodged in her throat as she tumbled headfirst down the steep, jagged metal stairs.

FOUR

Brady gave up trying to get comfortable on the blow-up mattress and instead observed the shark appearing to float far above him, visible through the portal beside his makeshift bed. The tank lights would be turned off in ten more minutes. A shame, really, because watching the ocean creatures in their blue world had a soothing effect.

The kids' whispers carried through the carpeted tunnel, and he wondered how long it would be before the sugar and excitement wore off. He shifted onto his side and became engrossed with the sea turtle who, because of buoyancy issues resulting from his accident, swam with his tail pointed to the ceiling. The turtle had captured the group's interest, and they'd peppered Olivia with questions. She'd been a wonderful host…patient, friendly and composed. He'd picked up on subtle signs of her distress—a flash in her eyes, a tremor in hand—only because he'd known what to look for. He had to give her credit for holding it together.

His lids fluttered closed, only to pop open at the sound of a terror-filled scream.

"Did you hear that, Captain?" Michael, bedded down a couple of feet away, scooted deeper into his sleeping bag.

"Stay put. I'm going to check it out."

Grabbing his flashlight from his pack, Brady instructed everyone to remain in place. Norman left his spot at the tunnel entrance and paced among the now quiet kids. Brady hurried through the space, expecting to encounter Olivia. But when he reached the end, he saw that her cot was empty.

Dread winged through him. He jogged through the hallway and poked his head into the women's restroom.

"Olivia? You in here?"

Not a single sound interrupted the socket lights' buzz. A sense of urgency gripped him. Calling her name, he continued down the hall and rounded the corner into the escalator area. The space was open to the second story and, thanks to the wall of glass, afforded an expansive view of the River Expedition building and waterfront. Striding beneath the twin escalators, he approached the doors.

A reflection in the glass diverted his attention. Pivoting, he probed the space with his gaze and realized the out-of-place shadow wasn't a trick of the light. It was a person, sprawled at the bottom of the steep escalators. Long black hair fanned across the shiny floor grate. A ribbon of dark liquid glistened beneath her cheek.

Olivia.

She wasn't moving.

Could she be—

Derek had been like that, too, his face locked in forever sleep.

Brady forced his leaden feet into motion. At her side, he fell to his knees and felt for a pulse. The breath whooshed from his lungs. Not dead.

Thank you, Lord.

"Olivia, can you hear me?" He searched for the blood source and discovered a deep gash behind her right ear.

She reacted to his probing fingers with an agonized moan. She flinched away from him, her pupils dilated in fear.

"It's me, Brady. I'm here to help."

Her forehead pinched. When she attempted to sit up, she hissed and cradled her arm against her chest.

Brady reached out but didn't touch her. "What happened?"

Glancing at the floor above, she grimaced. "Someone pushed me."

Moving to shield her from further threat, he gauged the distance of her fall. Anger bubbled beneath his skin. "Did you see who did it?"

"No."

Questions piled up, but he tabled them. She'd suffered a terrible fall and likely had a concussion. The prospect of internal injuries worried him. "Where else do you hurt?"

"I'm sore all over, but my arm aches when I move it."

"I'm going to call for an ambulance. In the meantime, we should wait somewhere more secure. Do you think you can walk?"

"No ambulance." She attempted to get up and faltered.

Brady gingerly placed his arm around her waist and helped her stand. She weaved on her feet and sank against him, her breaths coming in uneven bursts. His worry ratcheted up a notch.

"You're going to the hospital."

With her cheek pressed against his chest, she murmured, "Police and EMTs will end the kids' night on a sour note."

"There's no getting around that, Olivia," he said, his voice gruffer than usual. Her concern for the kids in this moment meant a lot.

"I'll answer the questions and fill out a report, just not here."

That she was continuing to lean on him was testament of her distress. Perceiving his unspoken wishes in the initial weeks of their acquaintance, she'd been careful to keep her distance. He hadn't noticed the differences in their heights before—the top of her head came even with his chin—or the sweet scent clinging to her skin. Or was it her shampoo?

Brady's hold on her tightened.

"I'll take you in my truck."

She straightened and edged out of his sheltering embrace, her eyes looking everywhere but at him. "The kids—"

"Norman and Dana will contact their parents to let them know what's happening. The field trip will be cut short, but they'll be safe in their homes. Maybe we can try this again at a later date."

He texted instructions to Norman to bring his pack and Olivia's phone, which she'd left on her cot. Brady guided her to a wooden bench and sat down beside her. Was her attacker hanging around to discover the outcome of his actions? The unknowns frustrated him. In real-life military missions, his objectives were clearly laid out and his adversary established. He had no idea if this person was aiming to scare Olivia or end her.

Despite the comfortable temperature inside the aquarium, a chill washed over him, raising the hair on his arms.

He extracted a clean cotton T-shirt from his pack and held it up. "This will stem the bleeding."

Not waiting for her response, he gently swept her hair behind her shoulder and placed the folded material against her wound. Her lips pressed together. "I know it hurts," he murmured regretfully. "I can't tell how deep the gash is, though."

She lifted her uninjured arm and held the material in place. "I hope this wasn't one of your favorite shirts."

"I'm not particular about what I wear." Growing up, he hadn't had the luxury of caring what he wore. His grandmother had purchased his scant wardrobe from the local thrift shop because that's all she could afford. Thanks to his career, he was either in flight suits, military-issue PT gear or dress blues. "Mind if I use your phone to call the guard?"

She told him where to find the contact information and listened as he relayed the problem. By the time Norman located Brady's pickup truck in the parking lot and drove it to the entrance, the guard was already there. This wasn't the same one who'd tried to evict him. Olivia introduced him as the head of security, Don Welch. With a broad face and heavy jowls, he reminded Brady of an English bulldog, the Marine Corps mascot. His eyes snapped, and lips pulled back over his crooked teeth.

Before they left, Norman reassured him that he would call all the parents and ensure the kids got home safely. Brady thanked him and assisted Olivia into the crisp night. Once she was settled in the passenger seat, he leaned in and fastened her seat belt, careful not to touch her injured arm. The forearm area looked pink and swollen. A quick glance at her face revealed her struggle to manage the discomfort.

Compassion, an emotion his parents' abandonment and military training had almost managed to mute, lodged in his chest. She didn't deserve this.

"I'll try to avoid the potholes and speed bumps."

He hurried to the driver's side and turned on the heater full blast. Despite his vow, he couldn't avoid every rough road surface. Relief flooded him when the hospital sign pointed them to the entrance. As it was after midnight, he was able to find a convenient parking spot.

He studied her profile draped in shadows. "Should I get a wheelchair?"

"I can walk."

"I'll be right beside you," he promised.

She turned to look at him, her brows forming a single line of surprise. Her lips parted, but no words escaped.

Brady could guess what was on her mind. Why hadn't he insisted they call an ambulance? He could've left her in the care of medical professionals and returned to his group. For reasons he couldn't explain, he hadn't even entertained that option.

Helping her out of the truck, he stuck close as they made their way to the brightly lit emergency room entrance. The slam of a car door shot through the night, and Olivia jumped.

"It's okay," he said, sliding his arm around her as he performed a quick scan of their surroundings.

Her throat convulsed. "I can feel his breath on my neck. His hand on my back, shoving me over the edge."

"The police will find this guy, Olivia."

Her expression said she wasn't convinced; her big, liquid eyes asked the question neither wanted to consider. *What if they don't?*

"You're a fortunate young woman." The ER doctor finished consulting his handheld tablet and gazed at her with bloodshot eyes. "You didn't suffer head trauma or internal injuries. As soon as your discharge papers are ready, you can go home."

The prospect of her soft, cozy bed should've sounded ideal. Home wasn't the same anymore, though. Not without Derek's larger-than-life presence.

A new thought, subtle and insidious, occurred to her.

Her attacker knew where she worked. Did he know where she lived, too?

Brady left the plastic chair to stand at her bedside. "What about her arm?"

"The swelling needs to go down before the fracture can be addressed." To Olivia, he said, "Your nurse will make an appointment to get your cast put on. The orthopedic clinic is closed during the weekend, so it will be Monday. We'll give you a sling to keep your arm stable until then."

The doctor left, and Olivia was alone with Brady again. His austere expression hadn't altered in the hours since their arrival, his laser-sharp gaze missing nothing. He'd remained by her side every minute, except for during the MRI, of course. The medical staff had barred him from entering the room. He hadn't been happy about that. Despite their non-relationship, she was glad he'd stuck around. Brady kept her grounded whenever the memories pressed in and panic threatened.

"Can I get you anything?"

His blue-gray eyes assessed her with polite courtesy. This was his professional persona, crafted to hide his thoughts and emotions. She'd seen him drop the protective shield around only one person, and he was gone.

When she didn't respond, Brady shifted, his hip nudging the bed as he stretched out his hand. He came short of touching her, however. "What's wrong?"

"Nothing." *Everything.*

"You're pale."

"I have a headache." Unable to stand his shrewd inspection any longer, she shoved the blanket off and swung her legs over the side, forcing him to move back. Her bruised ankle protested. "Would you mind handing me my clothes? I'm leaving the moment she delivers the paperwork."

He did as she asked. "There's a detective waiting to take your statement. If you're not feeling up to it, I can send him away."

"How long has he been out there?"

"He approached me during your MRI. I told him he'd have to wait."

She sighed. "I'll talk to him."

A half hour later, the interview had drained the last of her stamina. She was sore from the crown of her head down to her toes, and the lingering pain in her arm made her nauseated.

"That's enough for now, Detective Shaw." Brady opened the door to the hallway and delivered a pointed stare. "Olivia is overdue for some peace and quiet."

For once, she was grateful for the captain's observation skills. The silver-haired detective nodded in understanding and gave her a business card. "Call me if you remember anything else."

"Will you let me know what you find on the security feeds?"

"Absolutely. We'll also dust for prints on your original air cylinders. That may take longer."

Brady waited in the hall while she changed back into her uniform. The pants were ripped at the knee and streaked with dirt. The fabric smelled dirty, almost metallic. The sick feeling grew. It took the last of her energy to block the day's events. She wasn't about to break down in front of Brady.

He didn't bombard her with questions during the ride to the Marine Corps Air Station, a small base situated on the New River a few miles from the larger base, Camp Lejeune. The air station was home to the School of Infantry and the helicopter and tilt-rotor Osprey squadrons. There were also family living quarters, a commissary and

exchange, bowling alley, library and movie theater. It had
been her home for eighteen months. Seven of those she'd
shared with Derek. Sometimes it didn't seem possible that
he'd been gone nearly a year.

They approached the main gate manned with three
marines, and Brady entered the lane closest to the guard
hut. As he flashed his military ID and offered a greeting,
Olivia studied his face. The exhaustion he must be feeling
didn't show. There wasn't a hint of stubble on his chis-
eled jaw. No shadows beneath his eyes. His blond hair,
admittedly low-maintenance as short as it was, bore no
evidence of his shark tank swim.

She'd met him two years ago this month. Two years,
and they hadn't shared much more than shallow conversation. Now he was her self-appointed companion, an up
close witness to her fear, pain and vulnerability.

The darkness hid her grimace. Tomorrow, she promised herself. Tomorrow she'd feel stronger and better prepared to deal with the fact someone wanted her dead.

The streets were damp from a recent rain and the side-
walks empty. In her cul-de-sac, Brady pulled the truck
in to her driveway, killed the engine and stared out the
windshield. Unlike the other two-story duplexes around
them, hers didn't pay homage to the autumn season with
wreaths or pumpkins. The only personal touch was the
Marine Corps sign above the garage door. He and Derek
had nailed it up there together.

Brady didn't move. He didn't appear to be breathing.

She reached for the handle with her free hand. Her left
arm was tucked safely into a sturdy black sling. "Thanks
for the ride home. I'll call someone to pick me up on their
way to work in the morning."

He shook his head as if to shake off a stupor. "I'm not
leaving."

Before she could ask exactly how long he planned to stay, he'd exited the vehicle and ushered her to the porch. Taking her key, he unlocked the door and entered first, flipping on lights and performing a sweep of her home.

"Even if this guy has my address, he can't get to me here."

He peeked into the half bath tucked beneath the stairs and dodged a collection of cardboard boxes packed with books. "Not necessarily. He could be military or have contacts that would grant him base access. Civilians staff the commissary and other businesses. They have access, too."

Why hadn't she thought of that? Feeling light-headed, Olivia managed to reach the couch dominating the opposite wall and sink onto a broad cushion. She closed her eyes and waited for the dizziness to pass.

A blanket whispered over her. She lifted her head and was surprised to see Brady so close, tucking the corners around her shoulders. His blue-gray eyes, which she associated with bleak winter skies, reflected concern. Shocking.

Crouching before her, he proceeded to untie her tennis shoes and gently work them off her feet. Her mouth dried.

"Stay put." He straightened and strode to the kitchen.

Ordinarily, Olivia would've bristled at his authoritative tone. She certainly wouldn't have remained on the couch while he rustled around in her domain. But this wasn't an ordinary situation.

Warmth from the fuzzy blanket seeped into her aching, limp body, and her eyelids grew heavy. She curled into the sofa and was dozing off when he returned with a bowl of steaming soup. The aroma of chicken broth made her stomach growl.

"I heated up chicken noodle soup," he said, setting a

green soda can on the coffee table and handing her the bowl. "I couldn't find crackers."

"I didn't bother restocking the pantry since I'm moving soon."

"I noticed." His careful gaze slid over the bare walls studded with protruding nails before returning to her. "Do you need help eating?"

"I can manage," she croaked out. Brady spoon-feeding her? Not happening. "What about you? Wasn't there enough for two?"

He lowered his lean, athletic frame into the recliner and splayed his hands over the curved arms. He had nice hands, she noted. No rings.

"I'm not hungry."

She balanced the bowl on her knees and took several bites. "You seem comfortable taking care of the sick and injured."

His eyes became hooded. "My grandmother was frail when I first got there. By the time I was fifteen, she was barely mobile."

"That's a lot of responsibility for a kid," she said cautiously.

"I owed her."

A lump formed in her throat. Had his grandmother resented having to raise her young grandson? Had she made him feel like a burden?

Instead of voicing those questions, she kept the tone light. "What did you do for meals?"

"She taught me the basics."

"There weren't friends or neighbors to help out?"

His fingers gripped the leather until his knuckles went white. "My grandmother and I were basically on our own."

She could picture him as a gangly young teen, hiding

his hurting heart with defiant pride. Or maybe he'd been like he was now…polite to a fault, efficient and closed off. A loner determined not to give anyone the power to hurt him again.

Olivia now wished that she'd asked Derek how he'd managed to make friends with Brady. Knowing Derek, she thought fondly, he'd made a nuisance of himself until Brady had given in.

"You had to do the grocery shopping and house cleaning?"

"And pay the bills, when there was enough money to cover them, as well as the yard work and anything else that needed doing." He leaned forward. "That's enough about me. Let's talk about you, Olivia. Who would want to kill you and why?"

FIVE

He immediately regretted his bluntness.

Olivia set her bowl down without finishing the contents. Her hand shook as she gripped the soda can but didn't lift it to her lips.

"I can't answer that."

Brady's gaze catalogued the unhappy set of her mouth and the utter exhaustion clutching her features. This wasn't an ideal time to discuss theories. Being inside this place again had knocked him off-kilter. His mind kept returning to the pivotal conversation that had played out in this very room. The revelations Derek had shared—that he'd staged his own death to escape his mafia family and was using a fake identity—had threatened the foundations of their friendship. Derek had convinced him Olivia would be safer not knowing the truth. He could never tell her what he'd learned that long-ago day. What would be the point? Besides, he'd made a solemn promise to Derek that she'd never learn the truth from his lips. Unlike his parents, he honored his promises.

This is just for a short while, his mom had said, not meeting his gaze. *We'll come back for you as soon as we find a place to settle.*

"We can talk about it in the morning," he said, "after you've gotten a good night's sleep. Why don't you finish your soup and go on up to bed? I'll take the couch."

Shock pulled her lips apart. "You're not staying. There's no need—"

"You've suffered a concussion and other injuries."

"Minor injuries," she corrected. "The concussion is a mild one."

Brady left his chair and came around to her side of the coffee table. He removed his jacket and toed off his tennis shoes.

She lifted her face, her ink-colored hair spilling over her shoulders. "I'm safe here, Brady," she said, but her tone lacked conviction.

Sinking onto the couch, he shifted toward her and rested his arm across the back. "Until today, you thought you were safe at the aquarium."

Denial flashed in her eyes. He didn't blame her for resisting the truth.

"You shouldn't be alone tonight. Can you spend the night with a friend?"

"My best friend, Angela, lives in Wilmington. Even if I had the energy to make the hour trip, I wouldn't. She's due to have her first baby in another month. I won't bring this stress into her life. I have several friends from church, but it's the middle of the night. I don't want to bother them."

"Then it's settled. Go to sleep, Olivia."

She hesitated.

"I'll be as quiet as a church mouse. You won't know I'm here."

Sending him a disbelieving look, she got to her feet and retreated upstairs, only to return with a pillow and blanket.

Lying there in the dark, he let the memories of her and Derek wash over him. He couldn't recall witnessing a single argument between them. Despite Brady's conviction that she'd married Derek for the wrong reasons, the couple had appeared to be happy. Appearances weren't always accurate, though. Derek had proclaimed to be an ordinary Virginia native who loved baseball and hot dogs when, in fact, he'd been born into New Jersey mafia royalty. He probably hadn't even set foot in Virginia.

Brady had been shocked and angered by the deception. He'd gone so far as to argue the gross injustice Derek had inflicted on Olivia. Ever the smooth talker, Derek had defended his decision not to tell her. Their volleyed words circled around in his mind. Would Derek have second-guessed that decision if he'd known there was a ticking time bomb in his head?

With no answers forthcoming, he drifted into a troubled sleep. He was jarred awake by the creak of the storm door.

Leaping from the couch, he heard the knob rotate and regretted not asking Olivia where Derek's pistol was hidden. His head stuffed full of cotton and his vision blurry, he searched the sparse living area for a makeshift weapon.

The door swung inward, and a slim figure slipped through.

He was about to give the intruder a face full of Sheetrock when he noticed the plate of muffins.

Brady opened the blinds to let sunlight stream in. "What do you think you're doing?"

The sudden brightness startled the woman. She yelped and pressed her hand to her chest. "*You.* Captain something-or-other. What are you doing in Olivia's house?"

He recognized her freckles and wavy brown hair. Erin, the other diver. "She knows I'm here." Glancing pointedly at his watch, he said, "Do you make a habit of dropping by unannounced and letting yourself in?"

Sidestepping him, she plunked the plate onto the high, round dining table and held up a key. "I was on my way to work and thought I'd check on her. She keeps a spare key on the top window ledge." She crossed her arms. "How is she?"

Brady studied her, trying to gauge her sincerity. Was Erin here because she truly cared about Olivia? Maybe she felt guilty for what happened. Or maybe she was responsible.

She listened to him recount the doctor's diagnosis with a growing frown. "Nothing like this has ever happened at the aquarium. Does she have any idea who might've pushed her?"

"No, she doesn't." He wouldn't have shared that sort of information, anyway. "Do you?"

She shook her head with force, making her ponytail bounce. "Olivia is well liked and respected." Her attention swung to the stairs. "You're awake."

Erin crossed the room and enveloped Olivia in a loose hug. Olivia's gaze met his briefly before she eased out of the embrace and greeted her friend with a weak smile. She didn't look rested, he noted with dismay. Her fresh-from-the-shower appearance couldn't disguise the shadows under her eyes. He took in the faded blue jeans and snug turquoise sweater. Couldn't have been easy maneuvering with a broken arm.

She gestured, the sling flopping against her thigh. "Can you lend me a hand?"

Erin assisted her. "I brought breakfast. Is there anything else I can get you?"

"That was thoughtful." The women joined him beside the table. Olivia favored her sprained ankle. "I don't need anything else, but I could use a ride into work."

"The doctor told you to rest," Brady interjected.

"I'm on the schedule for today."

"I'm positive your superiors will understand. This has

the potential to be a worker's compensation nightmare. They'll want you to take your time and recuperate."

She stiffened. "I'm not going to *sue* the aquarium."

"He's right." Erin patted Olivia's shoulder. "Besides, I have to be there in a half hour."

After seeing Erin to the door and saying goodbye, Olivia turned and faced him. The light of determination in her eyes hadn't dimmed. "My work is important. I need to be there."

"Will your project be in jeopardy if you don't go in this weekend?"

She worried her full lower lip in a way that made it hard for him to concentrate. Why was he noticing these things? He wasn't allowed to be attracted to her. She was Derek's *wife*. He didn't approve of her. At least, he didn't used to. He wasn't sure what to make of her. The shallow label no longer seemed to apply.

"I suppose not, as long as Roman does his part."

She unwrapped the plastic and chose a muffin.

"Wait." He stopped her from taking a bite. "Erin could be the guilty party."

Her dark brows winging up, she shot him an incredulous look. "You think she poisoned the blueberries?"

"How well do you know her? You hold one of the senior positions. Is it possible she'd try to get you out of the way?"

"She does not want my job." Taking a large bite, she took her time chewing. "Erin works for the forestry department in the river building. The reason she helps out our aquatic staff from time to time is because she has her diving certification."

"What about pink-hair girl?"

"Maya? She's there for the paycheck. Her social life takes precedence over anything happening at work."

Brady pulled out a chair and motioned for her to sit. "What do you prefer? Juice or coffee?"

"Oh no. You're not playing host today." Limping past him, she led the way into the galley kitchen and popped a coffee pod into the machine with her free hand. "What do *you* prefer, Captain?"

"Coffee. Black."

He took stock of the boxes stuffed with pots and pans and wondered if she'd had help organizing the move or if she'd done it alone. His conscience poked him. What had his pastor been preaching about in recent weeks? Serving others, especially widows and orphans.

The aroma of rich coffee swirled around him. "Here you are."

Olivia had put his coffee into a paper to-go cup complete with lid. Hers, on the other hand, was in a ceramic mug.

"Subtle," he said.

She lifted her chin. "We agreed to go our separate ways once the field trip was over, remember?"

"That was before you took a plunge down the escalator."

"I'm not your responsibility, Brady. You can leave with a clear conscience."

Is that what he wanted? To leave and never look back? Strange, his answer wasn't as straightforward as it would've been twenty-four hours ago.

"Derek would want me to help you."

He realized that was the wrong thing to say as soon as the words left his mouth.

"You don't owe him anything, and you certainly don't owe me."

"Olivia—"

"In my experience, duty has two very different applications. Duty can be a calling, as in dedication to your country. That's the admirable kind. The same can't be said for when a person feels obligated to do something. My father stuck around, not because he loved and cherished my mom, but because it was his *duty*." Her nose scrunched and eyes snapped. "He made sure we all knew it, too. That duty is a burden, and I don't want any part of it." Brushing past him, she stalk-limped to the door and jerked it open. "Please, just go."

Feeling like a callous jerk, he paused on the threshold. "What happens if this guy breaches the base?"

"I'll handle it." Her posture warned him to back off.

"You have my number. Call or text anytime, day or night."

"Goodbye, Brady."

Sending Brady away had been the right thing to do. At least, that's what Olivia kept telling herself. She'd had many moments of doubt over the weekend. The nights were the worst. Every noise inside and outside her home held the potential of danger. Daytime wasn't much better, considering she had empty hours to fret over her predicament.

She'd assumed returning to work would improve her mood. During the day, the aquarium was a bright, cheerful space, and the visitors' excitement was catching. She hadn't anticipated how Friday's events would tarnish her perceptions. There were limitless spots for a criminal to hide and spy on her.

"Can we sign your cast, Olivia?"

The college-age girls working the gift shop register offered up shy smiles. Their undisguised curiosity matched that of the other staff members she'd encountered so far.

"Sure. You'll be the first."

Placing the pack of chewing gum on the counter and handing over a couple of dollar bills, she extended her arm. Roman approached while they were scrawling their names.

"Your accident has been the hot topic of the day." Behind the glasses, his eyes brimmed with concern, and for a moment, his mouth lost its characteristic scowl. "What happened exactly?"

Aware of the girls' keen interest, she shook her head. "I'll fill you in later."

"Right." Seeing a discarded marker, he held it up. "Do you mind?"

"Be my guest."

Roman drew a small, toothy shark, then signed his name beneath it.

Olivia grinned at the cartoonish likeness. "Nice."

"What can I say? I'm a man of many talents."

She told the girls goodbye and, grabbing her gum, left the gift shop with Roman. For a school day, there were a decent number of visitors milling around. Olivia had driven her car—dropped off by Erin and another coworker yesterday—to the ortho office midmorning. After getting fresh X-rays and a cast, she'd ordered lunch from a drive-through and driven straight here.

"No one's around to hear us," Roman said as they passed the jellyfish exhibit. "Did someone really push you?"

Menacing memories pulsed through her. The hot, ragged breath on her neck. The hand on her back.

"Yes."

Olivia scanned the exhibit areas, searching for anyone who looked or acted suspicious.

"What did the director say about you returning to

work?" He pushed open an employee-only door and waited for her to pass through.

"Ruth was gracious and accommodating. She didn't forbid me from returning, but she instructed me not to go anywhere alone."

They climbed the wide, spacious stairs without encountering other employees. The weak lighting and thick, austere cement walls hadn't bothered her before. Now the stairs struck her as a good place to corner someone. "The police weren't able to lift fingerprints from the air cylinders. They were wiped clean. The security cameras didn't offer a single glimpse of my attacker."

The detective had indicated that this guy had done his homework. He'd likely mapped out the camera locations and angles. That knowledge worried her. Her enemy was smart and methodical, which would make him harder to catch.

On the landing at the second-floor door, he paused. "Did Ruth promise extra security?"

Olivia nodded. "You know how seriously she takes her responsibilities. She won't compromise on the safety of her employees or aquarium guests."

"You can work without worrying then."

"I suppose."

Worrying was futile, of course, and she trusted God to protect her. She believed He had a plan for her life, even when that plan included losing her husband before their first anniversary.

The scriptures her mother shared with her during the funeral had stuck with her. *My brethren, count it all joy when ye fall into divers temptations; Knowing this, that the trying of your faith worketh patience. But let patience have her perfect work, that ye may be perfect and entire, wanting nothing.*

Trials…she seemed to be in a season of them.

When they reached their work space, located off the central entrance to the shark tank, thoughts of Brady bombarded her. He'd leaped into the water to save her.

She was still having trouble wrapping her mind around that.

To her surprise, the hours zipped past. She worked with a variety of people throughout the day, including Maya, who peppered her with more questions about Brady. Olivia was glad when the younger woman left for her dinner break. She was trying to forget him. Between his occasional terse texts, Maya's persistence and her own disobedient thoughts, she hadn't achieved that goal.

She delivered capelin to the penguins and realized it was a quarter of five. The twin buildings would soon empty of visitors and most of the staff. Outside, purple slowly crept across the horizon, obliterating the sunlight.

Olivia decided to retrieve her purse and ask a guard to escort her to her car. She and her current companion, Leon, were traversing the atrium area and chatting about his upcoming exams when a commanding figure entered her vision.

"Brady," she breathed.

He was talking to a greeter and hadn't noticed her.

Leon assumed she wanted his attention and called out. He twisted toward them. With a parting word to the greeter, he strode over.

Olivia couldn't read a single emotion in his face. It was a skill he must've started honing in elementary school. A boy who'd been cast off by his parents would've encountered harassment. By his own accounts, he and his grandmother had been dirt-poor. That would've added to his troubles.

She wondered what it would take to break through the barrier.

His gaze flickered to her cast. "I see you chose to co-ordinate with your uniform."

"I like blue."

"How's your pain level?"

"Manageable."

"And your ankle?"

"The swelling has gone down, and there's barely a twinge when I walk."

His eyes were solemn. Was he rehashing their last conversation? His pride might've taken a hit, but he couldn't have been hurt by her decision to send him away. Could he?

"I'm glad you're feeling better."

"Thank you."

Silence fraught with tension stretched between them.

"It's almost closing time," she said.

Why had he come? She'd answered his texts because he would've shown up on her doorstep if she hadn't. And having him around wasn't as terrible as she'd feared. It wasn't terrible at all, actually.

"Not gonna swim with the sharks, are you?" Leon quipped to Brady.

"I'll leave that to the professionals. Michael is convinced he left his Carolina Panthers sweatshirt here the other night. His dad gave it to him before he died, so it's of sentimental value. I promised I'd swing by after work."

He hadn't come for her sake.

Leon rubbed his hands together. "Olivia, can you take him? I have study group in an hour."

"Of course."

"Stay with her," he told Brady. "She's supposed to have an escort at all times. Director's rules."

He jogged away, leaving them alone in the middle of the giant atrium. Brady adjusted the watch on his wrist. "If you'd rather get someone else—"

"No, that's okay. I don't mind." Olivia started walking, and he fell into step. "Did you fly this weekend?"

As if he didn't get enough flight time on the job, he often took out his four-seater Cessna on weekends. He'd flown her and Derek to Charleston last summer. That was her first time in a small plane, and she'd been apprehensive. Derek had laughed off her concerns, but Brady had gone out of his way to ease her anxiety and make her comfortable. He'd explained every move before he did it. During the return flight, she'd actually relaxed enough to enjoy the scenery spread out below. Brady had noticed and flashed a brilliant smile solely for her benefit. It had been a rare moment of truce.

He nodded. "Yesterday."

"How was it?"

"Uneventful." He followed her into a stairwell. "As usual, it was good to see the world from a different perspective. I thought about asking you to come…thought you could use a distraction."

Olivia mulled over his words as they descended the steps. Considerate of her sore ankle, he matched his pace to hers.

"Would you have joined me if I'd asked?"

"It was a long weekend. I would've been tempted."

His expression was thoughtful as they reached the bottom level and entered the basement area. The stark gray cement walls and floors conjured thoughts of a mausoleum.

Brady's gaze took in the massive pumps and rows of salt sacks. "I'm surprised the lost and found is located down here."

"It's usually upstairs in the administrative offices. They're reorganizing, though, and temporarily storing files and other items in a supply closet."

Rooms along the interior wall stored everything from dangerous chemicals to toilet paper. The one she sought was in an out-of-the-way corner.

"Here we are." She opened the door and felt for the light switch. The halogen bulbs made popping noises as they flickered on. In the distance, a heavy door slammed. Brady turned and scanned the pump rows and the long, low hallway leading to other areas of the aquarium.

"Who typically works down here?"

"The operations officer. What color is Michael's sweat-shirt?" Olivia hurried past tall industrial shelving units on either side of the single aisle.

"Blue and black. Size twelve."

Several tubs bearing lost-and-found labels were stacked on the bottom row. Brady helped her maneuver them onto the floor. They each chose a tub and started rifling through decorated water bottles, stuffed animals and baby blankets.

"It's not in this one," she said.

"This one, either."

Together, they checked the third bin and came up empty.

Brady sighed and kneaded his nape. "Michael is going to be devastated."

"I'll ask the cleaning crew," she said. "I'm sure items don't make their way immediately here."

"I'd appreciate it."

The closet door closing didn't immediately cause panic. Olivia sidestepped the tubs and, striding past Brady, turned the knob, fully expecting it to respond.

"It's locked." She pounded on the door. "Hey! Let us out!"

Brady came up behind her and pulled out his cell. "I'll call building security."

"Don't bother." Sagging against the door, she wiped her hand down her face. "You won't get a signal. Not with these Fort Knox walls. Concrete is too thick."

Pocketing his phone, he leaned around her to inspect the knob. It was the kind that locked with a key from the outside. "Whoever closed the door had to have seen the light and heard us talking."

"The question is for what purpose."

"I can think of several," he said grimly.

Fear exploded in her chest. "My attacker could have used this opportunity to corral us until the building becomes a ghost town."

Then he'd return to finish them off.

SIX

"We're trapped." Olivia's throat convulsed. Horror dawned in her eyes. "Brady, I'm so sorry. You're in danger because of me. If Leon had brought you—"

"Hey, don't do that." He settled his hands on her shoulders. "You can't blame yourself. We're going to figure a way out of here."

Brady was perilously close to making a promise he couldn't keep. A quick survey of the closet revealed scant options. Unlike the pump area, this narrow room had a low ceiling—maybe nine feet in height—with a single air vent. There were no windows.

"How? There's no cell signal, and the bulk of the workforce has gone home." A quiver worked its way through her body like a mini earthquake. "We made it easy for him. I don't even know who he is or why he wants to kill me."

He gave her shoulders a gentle squeeze and worked to project confidence. "We'll hash out possible reasons when we're out of this box." Releasing her, he started inspecting the shelving contents. "Let's look for items that might help us."

"Like what?"

"Sharp, sturdy objects that we could use to break off the knob."

"Okay."

They didn't speak as they combed through cardboard boxes and plastic tubs. His nerves were on edge, his ears straining for any indication the enemy had returned. He heard Olivia yawn several times. Odd, considering the adrenaline rush she was likely experiencing.

Brady wasn't sure how much time passed before they reached the end of their search.

"Nothing," she exclaimed. "There's nothing here besides useless paper and clothing."

"If we can't get the door open, we can at least try and get someone's attention."

He located a box of neon printing paper he'd seen earlier and shoved the pieces, one by one, beneath the door. It wasn't his best idea, but he was out of options. His hope was that an employee would enter the pump room, see the scattered papers and come to investigate…*before* Olivia's attacker came back.

"We don't have a way to defend ourselves," she said. "Shouldn't we at least make it difficult for him to get in? We can use the tubs to block the entrance."

"Good idea."

Together, they scooted the tubs into position. Then they stacked cardboard boxes on top of them.

Kneading her temples, Olivia sat down on the floor and rested against the open wall space at the aisle's end. She yawned again. "I don't know why I'm so sleepy."

Brady was feeling sluggish, too. He joined her on the floor and contemplated his course of action when confronted with a knife or gun. Protecting Olivia was paramount.

"Tell me something." She pulled her knees up and wrapped her arms around her legs. "If you could go back in time and change one thing, what it would be?"

He looked over at her. "Don't do that. This isn't the time for regrets or confessions. We will get out of here alive, Olivia."

The words, as good as a promise, mocked him. What

was he *doing*? He couldn't guarantee their survival. While he'd received the best training possible to prepare him for dangerous situations, he was at a distinct disadvantage… cornered in an escape-proof room.

Her eyebrows dipped together, and she licked her lips. "Humor me."

He decided to be frank. "I wouldn't waste my tears on two people who never should've had a kid."

Her eyes were big and mysterious. "Have you ever attempted to contact your parents? Not for resolution, but for closure."

"Cynthia and Leo Johnson were what you'd call free spirits. They—we—traveled around living in tents or bunking with bleeding-heart strangers. They didn't have cell phones or email. That didn't change after they left, according to the postcards they sent. Guilt mail, I called it. The postcards arrived less and less frequently and ceased altogether a year later. Even if I'd wanted to speak to them, I wouldn't have had a clue how to reach them. I did receive word a few days after my eighteenth birthday. It was a letter from a hospital in California stating that they'd succumbed to injuries sustained in a fire. They thought of me before they died, at least. Giving the staff my grandmother's address."

Their deaths had suffocated any shred of hope he'd harbored that one day they'd beg for his forgiveness and another chance to be proper parents. He'd also been denied answers he would've sought eventually, answers he could've processed as an independent adult that he couldn't have as a disillusioned child.

"What about you?"

"I would relive Derek's last day." Her smile, the epitome of lost dreams, punched him in the gut. "I would've gotten up early and prepared his favorite breakfast. I would've gone to work late so we could share coffee and watch the sunrise. I would've hugged him—" her voice dropped to a whisper "—really hard. And thanked him for the time we had together."

An uncomfortable sensation filled his chest. "You loved him."

Her mouth twisted. "Why do you sound surprised? I wouldn't have married him, otherwise."

Brady dropped his gaze. He'd made a judgment call based on his own critical, skewed thinking.

"I can't believe this," she said slowly, her fingers curling into her palms. "You thought I was using him, didn't you? For what? Money? It's not like he was a trust-fund baby."

His guilt ballooned. Brady knew the opposite was true. Derek, a.k.a. Matteo Giordano, was a key member of a multimillion-dollar dynasty.

"Some girls lose their heads over marines, especially pilots. Derek was a magnet for the shallow, social-climbing type. He dated many of them but was never serious. Until you. Your relationship went from zero to sixty in no time flat, and I assumed you were like the rest."

Her face clouded. "You hurt him, you know. You were his best friend. He loved you like a brother. Because of your hang-ups, he had to walk a tightrope between us."

Shame blazed through him, leaving his skin hot and dry. "I admit I was unfair—"

She held up her hand. "You were wrong to judge me and wrong to shut me out. You didn't even give me a chance, Brady."

Turning her back to him, she huddled against the wall.

He felt like an ogre. The weight of his mistake became clear. He'd caused Derek and Olivia trouble, and there was nothing he could do to make up for it. He couldn't rewind time.

Lord Jesus, You're aware of my faults. I have a tendency to doubt others, to be critical. Please forgive me. Help me to...

Brady couldn't finish the prayer because his thoughts were becoming disjointed.

Beside him, Olivia curled up on her side, her cast an improbable pillow beneath her cheek. The crazy thing was that he wanted to nap alongside her. Somewhere in the deep fog shrouding his brain, a warning sounded. Something wasn't right.

He thought about getting a blanket from the lost and found for her, but his body wouldn't respond. The overwhelming urge to sleep forced him to the floor.

I'll just rest for a little while, and then I'll get her a blanket.

Brady's heart was going to explode.

He struggled to surface through the imprisoning fog. What was happening?

Think, Johnson.

The cold floor beneath him soothed his heated, sweat-coated skin. He pressed his hand against his chest in a vain attempt to slow his heartbeat. He felt like he'd just completed a twenty-five-mile marathon.

How long had he been out? Minutes? Hours?

Olivia.

With a grunt, he shoved onto his elbows. She was still curled onto her side.

Peaceful, he thought. *No, not peaceful.*

Red suffused her cheeks. Her forehead glistened. Her chest rose and fell rapidly.

Information clicked in his brain. Carbon monoxide poisoning.

He looked up and spotted the air vent.

The attacker wasn't coming back.

"Olivia." His voice lacked volume. Crawling closer, he shook her. "Wake up."

She didn't respond. There wasn't enough oxygen left.

He placed his shaking hand to her cheek, regret bitter on his tongue. "I should've given you the benefit of the doubt."

I'm sorry, Derek. By failing her, I failed you.

Colors faded from his vision, rendering the room in shades of gray.

Each breath was a fight for survival, each painful spasm of his heart a cry for more time.

Sorrow choking him, Brady lay down beside her and threaded his fingers through hers.

At least she wouldn't be alone.

Frantic voices disturbed her numbing dreams. A hard, plastic object covered her nose and mouth and refreshing air rushed into her lungs. Why was she sleeping on the ground?

Disoriented, she opened her eyes and encountered chaos. Men in uniforms rushed into the closet with medical equipment while others barked orders into their phones.

"You're awake." The woman crouched beside her inserted an IV. "Your name's Olivia, right?"

A gargled sound escaped. She couldn't seem to form words.

"No need to answer. Just breathe and let the oxygen do its work," she said, smiling. "I saw your name tag. You're going to take a ride to the nearest hospital, Olivia."

Hospital. Not again. She squeezed her eyes shut and searched her muddled mind.

She'd been talking to Leon when Brady showed up looking for something. A sweatshirt.

Brady!

It all came rushing back. The lost and found. This closet. Trapped.

Olivia's eyes popped open, and she started to sit up. "Where—"

A firm hand pressed her down. "Don't try to move. We're bringing in a stretcher for you."

She scooted her upper body in order to see past the woman, and a wave of denial washed over her. An unconscious Brady was being strapped to a backboard. He wasn't moving. Wasn't responding to oxygen.

He looked dead.

Open your eyes, she silently willed. *Please, Brady.*

Their last exchange couldn't be the final one. She'd been hurt and angry. Was *still* hurt and angry. More the former than the latter, truth be told. His opinion mattered. He didn't understand how much. He was so blinded by old wounds that he couldn't see his true worth. Or gauge his effect on others.

He didn't know that she craved his approval and friendship.

One of the EMTs working on him shook his head and said something to his partner. Their expressions were grave, as if they didn't expect him to make it.

Her heart quailed. Her chest ached. She hadn't given him a chance to apologize.

Brady can't die, Lord. Not because he's my last link to Derek and not because I'm the reason he's in danger. He's a good *man. A charitable human being. An honorable marine.*

The woman shifted to obscure her view. "Don't worry, your friend is being taken to the same hospital."

"What…happened?"

"From the looks of things, you've suffered carbon monoxide poisoning. The authorities will examine the ventilation system and determine the source of the malfunction."

Malfunction?

"Ah, here's your ride."

While Olivia was being strapped to the backboard, Brady was carried out of the room and to a waiting ambulance. Then it was her turn. A throng of bystanders watched the procession. She recognized the head of security, Don Welch. He was talking to the custodian, Mr. Ludwig. The EMTs walked at a fast clip. Since the straps prevented her from turning her head, she wasn't able to search for other familiar faces. Had the perpetrator hung around to make sure he'd achieved his goal? Would he conceal himself or remain in the open and pretend to be a concerned party?

Trying to answer impossible questions compounded the throbbing in her skull. After arriving at the ER, she was told Brady had regained consciousness and would spend time in a hyperbaric chamber, as would she. This would quickly replace the oxygen in their blood and tissues. Her immense relief was tainted by worry.

The attacker wouldn't be happy his plan was thwarted. He wasn't going to stop.

If he'd gotten to her inside the aquarium, he could get to her in the hospital. With staff, patients and visitors milling around, it would be easy for a criminal to blend in.

Surely Brady was out of danger, though. He'd simply been in the wrong place at the wrong time…right?

Olivia remained on high alert during her treatment. She studied every stranger who came near, trying to ascertain their motives. Help or harm?

When the nurse informed her that she would be admitted for observation, she balked.

"I can't stay here."

"It's standard procedure." She guided Olivia's wheelchair into the deserted hallway. "We'll need to measure your oxygen levels and other vitals throughout the night."

The prospect of spending the night in a sterile room, vulnerable to attack from a hundred different sources, was untenable. She kept her thoughts to herself during the elevator ride to the patient floor. Once in her room, she listened to the nurse's instructions without comment. As soon as she was alone, however, she located her bag of belongings, ducked in the bathroom and changed into her clothes.

The simple task left her light-headed. She exited the bathroom and immediately collided with a tall figure built of compact muscle. Firm hands closed around her upper arms and held her prisoner.

Olivia sucked in air and would've screamed if he hadn't spoken.

"I didn't mean to startle you."

"Brady?" She angled her face up and drank in his striking features. In the darkened room, his eyes appeared more blue than gray—tumultuous cerulean seas. She belatedly noticed he was wearing his jeans, T-shirt and hoodie. "You're dressed."

"So are you."

"You're leaving?"

His hands glided slowly down her arms and cast before falling away completely. "I'm going home, and I'd like for you to come with me. A buddy of mine has agreed to park outside my house overnight. He's Force Recon. Nothing will get past him. He's waiting downstairs to give us a ride."

Her throat clogged with emotion. Tears threatened. He'd almost died because of her. Overwhelmed, she walked to the bed and sat down, grateful her loose hair slid forward and hid her face.

Brady waited a beat before joining her. The thin mattress sagged beneath his weight.

"Look, I can't force you to come. I know you're upset with me and rightly so. But you should know that I have an alarm system, a comfortable guest bedroom and a freezer stocked with at least five different flavors of ice cream."

"I forgot about your addiction to dairy."

"I wouldn't want to live in a world without ice cream."

One tear escaped, then another. She folded her arms tightly across her middle and worked on not falling to pieces.

"Liv?" His voice was quiet. Hesitant.

"I'm okay," she gasped.

He scooted closer, until their arms and legs were touching, and very carefully swept her hair behind her shoulder. "No, I don't think you are."

That brought her head up. His intense gaze swept over her face. He frowned at the obvious tear tracks. Reaching behind him to the table on wheels, he snagged a tissue and held it out. His body heat warmed her, his nearness comforted her. What an odd reaction to the man she'd tiptoed around the duration of their acquaintance.

"I was wrong," he said quietly. "Words are cheap, I know, but I truly am sorry. You asked if there was anything I would redo in life. I'd like to change my answer. If I had another chance, I'd go back to the night we met. I'd welcome you with an open mind and congratulate Derek on his good fortune."

His remorse washed away the last of her anger. "I forgive you."

He tipped his head to the side. "Can we start over? As friends?"

"You did save my life. That has to count for something." Her attempt at lightheartedness wasn't entirely successful. "If not for your quick thinking, we wouldn't have made it."

"It wasn't our time," he said simply.

"You believe God orchestrated our rescue." The custodian, Mr. Ludwig, had come to the basement to retrieve paper towels and toilet paper. He'd seen the mess Brady had made by slipping papers under the door and come to investigate.

"You don't?"

"I…I believe He's in control. I've always taken comfort in that fact."

"But…"

She crushed the damp tissue into a ball. "I don't understand why this is happening, why He's *letting* it happen. I especially don't get why He'd allow you to be hurt, too." The image of an unconscious Brady would be forever burned into her brain. "You shouldn't be involved."

"Too late. I am involved." A sigh rumbled through his chest. "I *want* to help you, Olivia."

It was on the tip of her tongue to challenge him, to ask for a complete rundown of his motivations. She already knew the main reason… Derek. Was it the only reason? Did it matter?

He was an experienced marine, a living, breathing warrior. He was trained in hand-to-hand combat, weaponry and extracting himself from dicey situations.

Olivia would be a fool to send him away again.

SEVEN

Brady took her hand and didn't let go as they navigated the hallways. Because it was after midnight, the hospital had a hushed atmosphere, and there weren't many people around. He led her through a side entrance and straight into the back seat of a pristine black Mustang. Only then did he release her.

Olivia was certain her skin didn't *really* feel colder without his large, strong fingers enveloping hers.

The male driver twisted around to greet them. "That was fast."

Brady fastened his seat belt. "She was already dressed. Plus, we didn't bother with discharge papers."

"Don't mention that to Audrey." His attention switched to her. "Audrey's my fiancée, by the way. She's a surgical nurse in post-op. You must be Olivia."

"Hello."

She couldn't make out much in the darkness, but he appeared to be around the same age as her and Brady. His brown-black hair was shorn in the typical military haircut, and he had handsome features that hinted at his Asian heritage.

"Olivia, this is Sergeant Julian Tan."

"Right, the one with Force Recon."

"Did he happen to mention I'm not on an active team anymore?"

"He's an instructor," Brady told her. "He's careful to make that distinction, although I don't agree it matters."

"It's nice to meet you," she said.

"I wish it was under better circumstances. I met your husband a couple of times."

"Oh?"

"Julian joined us for basketball practice on occasion," Brady explained. "He used to go out on missions and couldn't be there for the actual games."

Julian nodded. "I'm sorry for your loss."

The sting of those words had become muted as the months marched past. She could accept them with grace instead of dissolving into grief.

Adjusting the vents in their direction, Julian faced forward and eased away from the curb.

Brady looked over at her. "You and Audrey have something in common. She found herself in a dangerous predicament about nine months ago, in this very hospital."

"Brady put his neck on the line for us," Julian supplied, taking the central artery through town.

"I gave you a set of keys and supplied you with fast food, that's all."

He snorted. "It was a lot bigger than that, and you know it."

"Mind if I fill Olivia in on the details later?"

"Be my guest. I'm sure she read about it in the newspapers, anyway." He met her gaze in the rearview mirror. "I wouldn't wish that kind of trouble on anyone else. I don't know the details of your situation, but I'm happy to help in any way I can."

"Thank you."

"First stop, base housing for essentials?" Julian asked.

"Yes, please," she said. "I can be in and out in under ten minutes."

Olivia stared out the window at the passing restaurants. They left the congested area behind and sped along the bypass leading to the air station. The mood inside the car changed almost imperceptibly. Julian sat straighter, his shoulders tightened and his jaw hardened.

Brady noticed, too. "What?"

"We have a tail."

Her throat started closing up. Her first instinct was to turn around and look out the rear window. Brady stopped her with a hand on her shoulder.

"Make and model?"

"Chevelle, a classic with serious engine power. Could be black or navy." Julian checked the side mirrors. "He's keeping a safe distance for now."

"We made the right decision to leave," she said.

"Yes, we did."

"Julian, are you armed? Because mine are under lock and key at the house."

"I came prepared. Let's test him," Julian said. "Hold on."

He jerked the wheel to the right and, zooming across two lanes, applied the brakes and took a sharp right. If not for his seat belt, Brady would've plowed into Olivia.

"Did we lose him?"

"Nope." Julian checked the mirrors. "He's not trying to hide anymore, either."

Brady finally looked back and muttered something unintelligible. Olivia did, too, and wished she hadn't. The older model car was deceptively large and clumsy looking, but it was quickly catching up.

"You recognize the car?" he asked her.

"No."

"Forget the air station," he said, facing forward again. "Let's lose him and go straight to my place."

"Roger. Time to shake this guy."

Julian gunned the gas, and the engine rumbled in response. Olivia was pressed against the leather seat as they raced through one sleepy neighborhood after another. Her pulse thundered in her ears.

Tension emanated from Brady in waves. His jaw was locked, his hands balled into fists.

A grinding thud vibrated through the Mustang, and she and Brady pitched forward. The Chevelle had rammed into them.

"Hold on!" Julian yelled.

He executed a sharp left turn onto a side street. In the middle of the turn, another jolt sent them spinning widely. An oak tree came rushing at Brady's door. Olivia screamed and seized his forearm, as if she could somehow protect him. At the last second, Julian righted the vehicle and hit the gas. They darted across the road and encountered uneven sidewalk. A garbage can went flying.

Olivia's stomach rolled. A bullet screamed through the rear windshield. Brady cupped her neck and shoved her down, his upper body shielding her as glass rained down.

"Okay," Julian spat. "*Now* I'm angry."

They were tumbled this way and that as the tires gripped the sidewalk, then air, then asphalt.

"Liv, are you hurt?" Brady's mouth hovered near her ear.

"Having trouble breathing, thanks to you."

His weight shifted an inch or so, but he continued to cover her. "Better?"

She nodded. "You okay?"

"I'm good."

Another bullet whizzed past them and embedded in the passenger seat headrest.

"Enough," Brady huffed. "Julian, your gun?"

The Mustang jerked left, then right in a zigzag pattern.

She heard the gun barrel's slide and click. Brady twisted, braced his back against the front seat and aimed. The instant Julian steadied the car, he began firing. The succinct pops assaulted her ears.

"One headlight gone," Brady called above the noise. "He's slowing."

"That's what I like to hear." Julian maintained speed.

Brisk air whipped through the car. Olivia slowly sat up and shook bits of glass from her hair.

"He's gone." Brady turned around the right way and sagged against the seat.

No one spoke as they navigated more side roads. Olivia tried not to think about what ways he might've attempted to kill them had they remained at the hospital. Her enemy was tenacious and inventive. She couldn't fathom what she'd done to inspire such hatred.

When they finally reached Brady's house and parked inside his garage, the damage to Julian's car became apparent.

She balled her right hand to stop the shaking. "I'll pay for the repairs."

Brady shot her an inscrutable glance across the hood. "No, I will. I involved him."

"Don't worry about it," Julian said. "That's what insurance is for."

Julian accepted his handgun from Brady. Under the garage lights, she saw that he was well over six feet tall and built like a tank. He would make a formidable adversary based on his physicality alone, never mind his intensive training as a Force Recon marine.

"Why don't you go get cleaned up while I inform the police?" Opening the rear door, he leaned in and examined the headrest. "The bullet he left for us might turn out to be useful."

"Thanks, brother." Brady ushered her inside and disarmed the alarm system, then started flipping on lights.

She'd been to his home a couple of times. Not much had changed. There were updated editions of architecture magazines stacked on the kitchen island and more kids' drawings hanging on his stainless-steel fridge. It was sweet that he not only kept them but displayed them in his otherwise pristine kitchen.

The combined living and dining areas—furnished with quality furniture pieces and lush throw rugs atop wooden floors—were similarly spotless. He took care of his possessions. Because he had so little as a child?

"You've lived here three years, right?"

"That's right." He opened the fridge. "Would you like a bottle of water? Soda?"

"Water, please." He passed it across the island. "You designed this house. Do you ever get the itch to move? Design another?"

He'd once said that, if he hadn't become a pilot, he would've pursued an architecture degree. Based on the functionality and comfort level of this house, she was confident he would've made a name for himself.

After guzzling down half of his own water, he considered her question. "I would change a few things about this place. Make the garage bigger and add more storage, for instance. Would I want to sell this one and start over from scratch? No."

Olivia wandered into the living room and gestured with her bottle to the French doors. "The courtyard area is my favorite part."

The split bedrooms were positioned to form a spacious stone courtyard, complete with grilling area, seating and koi pond. Brady had grilled steaks for her and Derek out there, and they'd spent hours beneath the stars. She'd been content to listen to the men recount stories about officer and flight schools.

He followed her and stared broodingly through the glass. Was he remembering those times, too?

Matching picture frames on the entertainment center caught her eye. They hadn't been there before. She studied the first one, which featured a pair of young marines on the tarmac with helicopters in the background, their arms slung around each other's shoulders and grinning like fools. Brady and Derek in the early years of their friendship.

Sensing Brady's perusal, she murmured, "You look like you don't have a care in the world."

He moved to stand beside her. "That was one moment of triumph and elation in the midst of crazy hard times."

"I enjoyed the stories about your escapades."

"I wouldn't have finished without Derek. My grandmother died six weeks before graduation, and I almost quit. He refused to let me."

She turned her head. "He was your closest friend, wasn't he?"

His lips lifted in a self-mocking smile. "I determined at a young age that being alone was better than caring about someone who'd eventually leave. I succeeded in my goal all through middle and high school. College was about studying and earning top marks. There wasn't time or energy to make friends in officer candidate school. And then, the first day of flight school, this cocky guy strolls up and starts chatting about cars, girls and everything else under the sun. Derek decided he was going to be my friend. I wasn't really given a choice."

Something occurred to her then. For a man like Brady,

who'd been discarded and ignored and who'd forged through life alone, a friendship like the one he'd shared with Derek would be worth safeguarding. And he had, hadn't he? He'd condemned her from the start, not giving her a chance to prove she was trustworthy. In Brady's mind, she'd appeared suddenly in Derek's life and become a fixture practically overnight. That hadn't helped her case.

Picking up the second frame, she tapped the glass. "Your grandmother?"

"Yes." His brows drew together. "That was taken the summer I went to live with her."

The towheaded boy in the photo was all angles and sharp edges. He didn't have the healthy roundness most boys that age possess. He was unsmiling, of course, and his eyes bore witness to desolation. His grandmother was as gangly and thin as Brady. Life experience had carved a network of lines around her mouth and eyes.

"She had a kind face." When he didn't reply, she said, "*Was* she kind?"

His chest rose and fell in an exaggerated sigh. "Yes, she was."

He was exhausted. Because of that, his guard was lowered, and emotions played across his face in quick succession. It was clear he missed her. Whatever sort of relationship they'd shared, he'd loved her. And now two people he'd risked his heart on were dead.

The need to offer comfort and companionship lodged deep in her chest. The forcefulness of it stole her breath. How many times had this man been held? Comforted? Loved? That last word startled her. She turned away before she damaged the tenuous connection that had formed between them.

Olivia had treasured friends in her life. She had sisters

who infuriated and delighted her, parents who loved and supported her, and a boisterous network of aunts, uncles and cousins. She was blessed.

Still, there was something about Captain Brady Johnson that called to her.

Brady liked having Olivia in his home. He'd experienced a brief burst of apprehension when she'd first walked inside. More than a year had passed since she'd been here, and not alone.

What he didn't like was her looking at him like he was a lost, helpless puppy that needed saving. It made him feel vulnerable, and he avoided that feeling at all costs.

"Which one do you like best?" Standing at the center island, a bowl cupped in one hand, he motioned with his spoon.

"It's impossible to choose." Seated on one of the stools, she shook her head. "You shouldn't have given me all five flavors."

He took another bite. "It's three o'clock in the morning. We shouldn't be eating anything. Why not go all out?"

They'd both showered and changed. Since she didn't have clean clothes with her, he'd lent her plaid pajama pants and a long-sleeved shirt. They hung on her smaller frame, but at least she was warm. Her hair was a sleek curtain down her back, and the military-green shirt complemented her skin and dark eyes.

The door to the garage opened, and Julian strolled inside as he was completing a call. "The police will be here in about twenty minutes to take our statements. They're almost finished processing the scene of our collision."

"Don't both of you work tomorrow?" Olivia said, glancing at the stove clock. "I mean today?"

"I'm used to functioning on little or no sleep." Julian

clapped him on the back. "Watch out for this one, though. He gets giddy when he's sleep deprived."

Brady rolled his eyes. "I have no idea what you're talking about."

"You know when you're exhausted and you get delirious and laugh at stupid stuff?"

Olivia smiled. "Brady does that?"

"No, I don't." Out of the corner of his eye, he could see Julian nodding his head. "Fine. No ice cream for you."

"Why would I want your ice cream when I can have Audrey's pancakes?" To Olivia, he said, "We live in the same apartment complex, on the same floor. She invites me over for breakfast most days."

"She spoils you." Brady waved his spoon at him. "And I suppose you earned a scoop or two of ice cream considering you got us here alive."

"A scoop or two, huh?" After grabbing a bowl from the cabinet, he opened the freezer and considered the contents. "I'm thinking more along the lines of a year's supply."

"You're out of your mind, Tan."

Brady looked up to find Olivia watching their exchange with a bemused expression. Maybe it was the late hour or the sugar rush, but he allowed himself to fully appreciate her beauty. Hers wasn't cool or manufactured. It was vibrant. Natural. Her inner effervescence was reflected in her bright eyes and sweet smile.

Julian shattered his musings when he perched on a stool near Olivia's. "Speaking of our harrowing ride home, any ideas who's behind this?"

Her eyes took on a hunted look. "I don't have any work rivals that I'm aware of. I'm not involved in workplace disputes."

"What about the aquarium?" Julian said. "Are there

any repeat visitors who stand out in your mind? Anyone who might've paid you undue attention?"

"I can't think of anyone." Going to the sink, she rinsed out her bowl and turned to face them.

Brady finished off his ice cream and joined her at the sink. "Why don't you tell Julian about your special project with the saltwater fish?"

Scooting over to give him room, she outlined the project's goals of raising saltwater fish in-house and lessening the need to gather wild specimens.

"Would this project threaten the businesses that supply saltwater fish?"

"It doesn't work that way. We either get fish from other facilities or teams of aquarists travel to the ocean once or twice a year and catch wild populations," she said. "Roman is my partner on this project. Why isn't he being threatened?"

"You indicated that you're the one in charge, not him. He follows your lead. With you out of the way, the project falls apart."

Julian returned to the freezer for second helpings. "Let's look at it from a different angle." He set the half-gallon tub on the counter. "Do you have any admirers in your life? Someone interested in romance?"

Brady opened his mouth to refute the idea. Everyone knew she was in mourning. But the expression on her face stopped him.

"The aquarium vet, Dr. Zach Ledford," she said, absently pushing her fingertips between the cast and her skin. "He asked me out, and I declined."

"Seriously?" Brady demanded. "Does he not know about Derek?"

Her lashes swept down. "He knows."

"Everyone grieves at their own pace." Julian shot him

a warning glance. "He might've assumed you were ready to date again."

Brady watched as she continued to try to ease the itch beneath her cast. "Was he upset when you told him no?"

"He said he understood, but I got the impression he was annoyed."

Julian leaned against the island. "While most guys don't enjoy rejection, they deal with it and move on. Some hold grudges."

"And that's a motive for murder?"

"It is if he's become obsessed and doesn't want anyone else to have you." Brady reached out and linked his fingers with hers, stilling their movement. "Do you need an antihistamine? We can't have you roaming the house hunting for pencils or wire coat hangers."

She winced and nodded. "The itching is becoming more noticeable."

"You kept the cast dry in the bathroom?"

"I wrapped it in the plastic bag you gave me and taped it up."

"Good." He fetched the medicine from his bathroom and poured her a glass of water. "Here you go."

"Thank you."

Brady intercepted Julian's speculative glance and raised eyebrows. He didn't want to begin to guess what his friend was thinking. He hadn't shared his reservations about Olivia with anyone other than Derek. In fact, he'd said very little about her. Julian was probably wondering how he'd gotten involved and why he'd chosen to stay involved.

"What do you know about Dr. Ledford?" he said.

"Zach's a competent and caring vet. He's been on staff for about six years, I think. I don't know much about his personal life besides the fact he's single."

"Has he asked other employees out?"

"If he has, I haven't heard about it. I honestly don't think Zach's a bad guy. His behavior toward me hasn't changed since I turned him down. He's still the friendly, laid-back guy he's always been."

He and Julian shared a glance. Evil wore many faces.

The doorbell chimed, and Olivia tensed. Brady touched her arm. "I'll let the police know we're both running on fumes, and that they'd better make it quick."

"Let them do their job." She shrugged. "The sooner they catch this guy, the sooner you and I can resume normal life."

Normal life? What would that look like now that they'd agreed to a fresh start?

As Brady made his way to the front door, he admitted that he wouldn't like going months without seeing or speaking to Olivia. What she wanted, however, was a mystery.

EIGHT

Olivia bolted upright in the strange bed. Her heart thudded against her rib cage. Had she heard actual gunshots? Had they been part of her nightmare or was there a gunman on the property?

Late afternoon sunshine streaked through the open blinds of the guest room.

Her eyes gritty, she shoved off the heavy maroon coverlet and tiptoed toward the door.

A floorboard creaked, and Brady arrived in the doorway. "Olivia? You okay?"

She stopped short. "I thought I heard gunshots."

"Gunshots?" he repeated, his brows drawing together. "You must have been having a nightmare. I heard you talking. I thought you were on the phone, but you must've been talking in your sleep."

He leaned against the frame and ran his fingers through his blond hair, further messing the short, disheveled strands. One cheek was pink and creased from his pillow, and his eyes were bloodshot. His soft cotton T-shirt was wrinkled. Striped socks peeked from beneath his jeans.

She liked seeing this less formal side to him, liked seeing hints of vulnerability. Her gaze roamed over his face, noting for the first time the pleasing symmetry of his features—the cheekbones that could cut glass, the tough angle of his jaw, the slight dimple in his chin and the full, pleasing mouth that balanced his inherent masculinity.

Olivia reached behind her to clasp the footboard and closed her eyes. This was ridiculous. Most likely a product of the strange events and serious lack of sleep.

"What's the matter?" He entered the room and, coming close, pressed his palm to her forehead. "Are you dizzy? Feverish?"

She looked up. "Your eyes are blue today, the same hue of the wildflowers in my grandmother's yard. Fringed bluestar I think, is their name."

He slowly lowered his hand. "What?"

Feeling silly, she said, "Um, sometimes your eyes are gray like winter skies. Other times they're blue."

"Yours are always brown."

The way he was looking at her sent a strange yearning arrowing through her. Her mouth went dry. "I know. Boring, right?"

"Not possible. You have beautiful eyes, the rich color and exquisite shape…" He swallowed hard and glanced at his watch. "I, uh, think we should eat. It's been about twelve hours since we had anything, and that was ice cream."

"Agreed."

Getting food into their systems would prevent any more odd exchanges. When she was ready to risk her heart again, she would never choose Brady, not with their history. And he would never choose her.

He rummaged through the fridge and pulled out a brown package and several peppers and onions. "How do you feel about pasta and meatballs? I don't have salad, but I do have garlic bread in the freezer."

"Comfort food. I'll take it." Quickly braiding her hair and securing it with a band, she washed her hands. "Where do we start?"

He located two cutting boards, and they worked, side

by side, chopping vegetables. It was a mundane chore that she hadn't dreamed she'd share with him.

"Have you told your family what's been going on?"

Her knife slowed. "Not yet. My sisters would insist on coming here." Her older two, especially. Jaqueline and Farrah would argue over who could protect her better. They argued about everything.

"If one of them were in trouble, you'd want to know."

She reached for another pepper. "I can't put them in harm's way."

"Are you close?"

"We've had our fair share of squabbles over the years, but nothing major. We air our differences of opinions and hug it out."

"I used to imagine what it would be like to have a big family," he mused. "Sometimes, when I was especially lonely, I daydreamed about my parents returning with younger siblings."

Olivia hid her surprise at the shared detail. "You don't have extended family?"

"My mom was an only child and orphaned at an early age. My dad's older brother died before I was born. He didn't have kids."

"Your grandmother didn't have siblings?"

"A few, scattered around the country and in no shape to travel."

"Growing up in our area of the Qualla Boundary, which is land owned by the Eastern Band of Cherokee Indians, adults took responsibility for kids whether they were related or not."

Brady actually smiled at her. "It takes a village to raise a child."

The smile transformed his face. She averted her gaze and focused on her task. A companionable silence filled the space as they prepared the meat sauce and noodles. He used a music app on his phone to play French cooking music and made her promise not to tell anyone, especially Julian, or he'd never hear the end of it.

When it was time to eat, Brady bowed his head and said a poignant, humble prayer that brought tears to her eyes. Derek had professed to be a Christ-follower and had attended church services, but he hadn't prayed with her. Not once. They hadn't shared the same spiritual values, and it had caused rifts in their relationship.

Olivia began to pose questions, personal ones, about his faith. Brady didn't divert the conversation or raise his guard. He answered each one with frank honesty. He didn't like discussing his childhood, but he had no problem sharing his walk with God. By the time their plates were cleared and the bread basket empty, she realized she'd learned more about him in one sit-down dinner than in two years of knowing him.

Her phone rang as he was clearing the table. Her good mood vanished. "It's Detective Shaw."

He resumed his seat across from her. She ended the call and set her phone down.

"The heating and air employees did a thorough examination of the basement system. It's in prime working condition."

"It's what we expected."

She twisted her hands together on the table surface. "They did find something unusual in the vent—long tubing with a nozzle."

His face flushed. "To attach to a carbon monoxide canister, right?"

"That's their assumption. Shaw called around town and located a welding company who'd recently had a canister stolen. Unfortunately, they don't have surveillance cameras."

"Any prints on the tubing?"

"Wiped clean."

"The bullet could provide valuable intel."

"This guy is good, Brady. Smart. Thorough." His resourcefulness could prove their downfall. "I doubt that the gun or the car belonged to him. He probably stole both."

He encased her hands with his own, warming them. "He'll make a mistake. They always do."

But would it be too late for them when he did?

The presence of military police outside her home should've put her at ease. After Shaw's call, Brady had driven her to the air station's provost marshal's office. They'd informed them of recent events and, to her surprise, received the promise of protection for the rest of her stay in base housing, and now she was back home. But her enemy had devised creative ways to reach her, and she worried he might decide to take out a marine in order to achieve his goal. She knew that Brady wasn't completely at ease, either. He'd told her that if he'd been able to bow out of today's flight training, he would've.

Pushing aside her concerns, she tackled the task she'd been procrastinating…deciding what to do with Derek's clothes. She planned to keep one camouflage uniform and most of his Marine-issued T-shirts. The rest would go to charity, she supposed.

Asking the Lord for strength, she entered their walk-in closet and began removing shirts and pants from hangers, folding them and making neat stacks on the bed. His scent had faded over the course of time. She was nearing the end of her task when she discovered a thick piece of paper in one of his pant pockets. Unfolding the smooth paper, she skimmed the printed article about a string of crimes in New Jersey. How strange. Why would Derek be interested in this, and furthermore, why would he keep it? Thinking it might be connected to his work somehow, she decided to ask Brady.

Her foot connected with a stack of decorative storage boxes and knocked them over. When she bent to restack them, her gaze fell on a shiny object in the carpet. Her eyelids prickled.

Derek's dog tags.

She let them dangle from her fingertips, the engraved letters catching the light.

They were supposed to go to Brady, she remembered with a start. Derek had been clear about what should happen to certain possessions should anything happen to him.

Closing her fist around them, she brought them to her chest, reliving the somber instructions. His preoccupation with death had been at odds with his carefree personality. She'd assigned it to his career's inherent dangers. That, and his other quirks. He'd insisted she keep her maiden name, Smith, instead of taking his surname. Social media accounts were taboo. He'd preached the importance of online security and had advised her not to share photos.

She glanced at the clock. Brady had texted that he'd be returning from a flight around 1700 hours. If she hurried, she could get the dog tags to him before he left the air station. And she could ask him about that article.

After changing into jeans and buttoning a jewel-toned sweater over her shirt, she grabbed her phone and keys, locked the front door and strode down the driveway. The driver's door of the police car swung open, and a female marine who'd reported for the afternoon shift stepped out. Of average height, she had big green eyes and vivid red hair pulled back into a braided bun. She introduced herself as Corporal Baker.

"Everything all right, ma'am?"

"I was wondering if you'd drive me over to the hangars. Captain Johnson is returning from a flight soon, and I need to see him."

The corporal considered her request, indecision playing over her gamine features.

"It shouldn't take long." Hooking her thumb over her shoulder, she said, "I'm not used to being confined to the house. The walls are starting to close in."

Understanding flashed. She motioned with a tilt of her head. "Hop in, ma'am."

"Thanks. And please, call me Olivia. I'm guessing we're around the same age."

Her smile was rueful as she climbed behind the wheel. When Olivia was buckled in, she said, "I'm Catriona. Off-duty, most people call me Cat."

"Your accent isn't local. Where are you from?"

"Chicago." Turning out of their neighborhood, she drove slowly past the old building that housed a bowling alley. "What about you?"

"On the other side of the state. I was born in Cherokee."

"I've been planning to visit the mountains ever since my transfer four months ago. I haven't found the time."

"The national park is worth the trip," Olivia said. Cat navigated the two-lane road winding through the base. The car chase forefront in Olivia's mind, she continually checked for cars in the rearview mirror. "Were you stationed in California?"

"Okinawa." Her fingers tightened on the wheel, and her lips thinned.

Olivia fell silent. She recognized the signs of distress.

Whatever happened at Cat's last duty station, she didn't want to talk about it.

"Well, I hope you like living here," she said. "If you enjoy the outdoors, specifically the water, you won't get bored."

The brim of Cat's cover cast her forehead and eyes in shadow. "I have no complaints so far," she said lightly. Turning into the squadrons' parking lot, she pulled around to the first building and cut the engine. "I'll walk with you."

Olivia nodded, suddenly bombarded with bittersweet memories. Family days were hosted here whenever the guys returned from missions. Welcome home days were special.

A door on their right opened, and a stocky, silver-haired gentleman emerged from the building. His face lit with surprised pleasure.

"Olivia!" Striding over, he gave her a quick hug. "It's good to see you."

"You too, sir." Lieutenant Colonel George Russell had been Derek's commanding officer. The squadron leaders encouraged off-duty socializing, and she'd spoken with him on multiple occasions at the officer's club.

"None of that. Call me George." His gaze assessed her in the gathering darkness. "How are you doing?"

He was talking about Derek, of course. "It's a process. Good days and bad, all mixed in together."

"He is missed."

She swallowed a lump in her throat.

"You broke your arm?" he said, nodding to the cast peeking out from her sweater.

"Yes. At work." She had no desire to recount the awful turn her life had taken.

George belatedly noticed Cat's presence. "Is there anything I can help you with, Olivia?"

"I'm here to see Brady."

"He and the others should be flying in shortly. Why don't you come with me?" He smiled kindly. "I'll take you to the flight line so you can watch them."

Cat remained with the patrol car as the Lieutenant Colonel ushered Olivia through the massive hangar that housed Huey helicopters. Since the flight line was restricted, he told a sergeant to inform the guys upstairs that they had an approved visitor.

They took up position at one end of the yawning opening that led out to the tarmac and runway. On her left, tiltrotor Ospreys were parked in a uniform line. To her right, there was another hangar and more helicopters, framed by pine woods.

While they waited, she asked George about his wife and new grandbaby. Pride filled his voice as he spoke about being a first-time grandfather.

"Here they come," he said, nodding to the orangesicle sky above the distant New River.

She counted four AH-1 SuperCobra attack helicopters.

"Captain Johnson has been quiet in recent months," he said.

"Quieter than usual? I didn't think that was possible."

"When he's not busy with his charity work, he attends our after-hours gatherings because he knows it's expected. He sticks to himself, though."

"Derek was the brother he never had."

"They were tight, all right. Of course, he hasn't let it affect his work. I've kept an eye on him. His instincts haven't wavered. His flying ability is top-notch."

According to Derek, Brady had set high standards for himself in high school and college. That drive had carried over to his military career and had made him into one of the best pilots Derek had worked alongside.

But career achievements couldn't take the place of human connection and meaningful relationships. With his best friend gone, Brady had likely closed himself off even more.

The distinctive thump of the rotator blades rippled the brisk air. She gathered her sweater lapels closer together as, one by one, the gray twin-engine helos landed on the tarmac. The blades slowed and the evening air eventually stilled. The marines began to disembark. Even with his helmet hiding his fair hair, she picked him out from the rest. There was no mistaking the lean build, erect posture and impatient stride. He and his weapons officer removed their helmets and started toward the hangar, conversing on the way.

The sunset's last hurrah washed him in iridescent light, highlighting his gorgeous facial structure and rendering his hair liquid gold. His olive-green flight suit showed off his broad shoulders, thick biceps and slim waist. Olivia stood immobile, engrossed in him. She couldn't look away. It was as if she'd been in a semi-awake state for eleven months, going through the motions but not truly alive. And now, suddenly, she was awake again. Colors were richer. Smells more complex. Sounds more nuanced.

Olivia tracked his approach, her tongue glued to the roof of her mouth.

Why him, Lord? Why now?

Guilt slammed into her. It was too soon. *Brady* thought it was too soon. His reaction to Zach's interest in her was swift and complete. He would be appalled if he knew she was seeing him in a new light.

I'm sorry, Derek. I had no idea I'd find myself in this

strange place…thinking your standoffish best friend is attractive.

She could—and would—ignore it.

When Brady finally noticed her, his brows slammed together and his gait quickened.

"Olivia, what's wrong?"

"Nothing's wrong. I found something of Derek's that he wanted you to have." Aware that Brady hadn't greeted his commanding officer because of his concern for her, she glanced at George.

Brady corrected his oversight and saluted the other man.

"Was it a good mission?" George asked.

"It was successful, sir." Brady answered his superior, but his blue-gray gaze remained fixed on Olivia.

George put his hand on her shoulder. "It's good to see you." To Brady, he said, "Bring Olivia to our next gathering. The other guys and their wives would love to catch up."

"Yes, sir."

When he was out of earshot, Brady lifted his hand to show her a thick folder. "I have to drop this off at the other hangar. Walk with me?"

She fell into step beside him and tried desperately not to notice his enticing cologne. "I didn't mean to startle you."

"I thought there might've been more trouble." He adjusted the bulky brown flight vest worn over his suit. "You didn't come here alone, did you?"

"Corporal Baker brought me."

They left the large tarmac behind, walked along a narrow strip that linked the hangars and entered another tarmac area. This one was smaller and held about half a dozen helicopters.

"You said you found something?"

She stopped, and he did, too. "Hold out your hand."

His forehead furrowing, he did as she instructed. Closing her fingers over the dog tags in her pocket, she was about to pull them out when a distant pop splintered the silence.

The next thing she knew, Brady was shoving her to the ground and shielding her with his body.

Bullets dug into the asphalt.

Her enemy had breached the base.

NINE

Another bullet whizzed over their heads with inches to spare.

They had to seek cover.

Brady latched onto Olivia's hand and tugged. "Let's go!"

They scrambled to their feet and, together, dashed to the nearest barrier, an aircraft tow tractor. Not ideal. He needed to get her to the hangar, but it was too far away. Too much open space between them and safety. The buildings' exterior lights were flickering on, thanks to the deepening shadows.

"Where is he?" she demanded, hunkered beside him. "The woods?"

"Yes."

He cringed when glass exploded. There went the tow vehicle's windshield. This guy had a high-powered rifle, and so far, no one else was aware of the attack. The hangar was empty, and any guys still in the office hadn't heard it. There was no reaction from the more distant hangars. No alarms sounding. They were on their own.

"Stay here."

She wouldn't release his hand. "Where are you going?"

"I'm going to get the door of the tow tractor open. If the keys are in the ignition, we'll try and drive out of range."

She licked her dry lips. "Okay."

"You have to let go," he reminded, lightly squeezing her hand.

She instantly released him.

"Remember, make yourself as small as possible."

He crawled along the length of the short, squat vehicle and, keeping his body behind the frame, quickly unlatched the door. Another shot blasted through the air, and the mirror attached to the door he'd just opened burst into pieces.

Olivia cried out.

Heart racing, blood boiling, he peered into the cab. No keys.

Thumping his fist against the frame, he probed their surroundings for another option. They needed an exit strategy.

His gaze swept over the woods. Ten, maybe fifteen steps and they'd be there. The shadows were thicker, and the tight network of trees would hinder the shooter's accuracy.

"We have to run," he told her. "He hits the gas tank on this tractor or one of the helos, things get messy fast."

"I trust you, Brady."

He couldn't begin to measure the magnitude of that statement. "We stick together."

She took his outstretched hand. At his nod, they bolted across the tarmac. Time slowed. Bullets pelted the tow truck, then shifted to the trees they were running toward. Bark splintered nearby.

They entered the wooded area and headed away from the hangars. The ground was soft from recent rain, and Brady worried that her sprained ankle would give way. Weaving between the trees in the dark, not being able to see the terrain, was an added hazard.

The onslaught temporarily ceased as the shooter gave chase.

Olivia clung to his hand with an iron grip. "The marina's not far from here," she said, her breaths coming in spurts.

The marina had a rental space with kayaks and other water-sports equipment. "If we can take cover inside the building, I can get out a call or text to the air control tower."

The report of a rifle echoed through the understory. The limb above her head cracked and swept down. Olivia yelped and ducked. She lost her footing and would've fallen if he hadn't hooked an arm around her waist and tugged her behind the tree. She gripped his shoulder to regain her balance.

In the distance, a siren wailed. Was that for their emergency or someone else's?

Either way, it could spook the shooter.

They turned and forged ahead. Despite her injured ankle, Olivia kept pace with him. They encountered a stream and splashed through the icy water. He tripped on a jutting root and caught himself on the bank. A jagged, broken-off limb gouged into his palm.

Olivia heard his exclamation. "You okay?"

He shook off the pain and clambered up the other side. "Fine."

Minutes later, they jogged across a deserted road and entered the waterfront park. The playgrounds sat silent, the parking lots empty. This place wouldn't be busy until spring.

"There." She pointed to the outline of a long, rectangular building. A single electric pole shed light on cement picnic tables and short docks extending into the river.

He led her in a circuitous route, keeping to the shadows.

They were almost to the building when a window shattered. Olivia shielded her head with her arms. Brady put his arm around her shoulders and guided her around to the back. Rows of yellow kayaks hung suspended on wooden frames. He heard shoes pounding the pavement.

Olivia stiffened. Brady steered her into the tight space between the frames and put himself between her and the shooter. Seconds dragged into minutes. Terrible tension built in the air between them, on the verge of exploding. His muscles quivered with suppressed energy.

A rock skittered past them. A strangled sound emanated from her.

Brady inched closer. He slid his uninjured hand beneath her braid and cupped her nape. His cheek grazed hers. "Shh."

She clutched either side of his waist, fingers bunching in the material. Her fine, vanilla-scented hair tickled his chin. Being this close to her was highly distracting.

Another footfall. Closer this time.

Could Olivia hear his heartbeat? Could the enemy? Because it was a roaring thunder in his ears.

He had to act. Had to do something. If the shooter discovered their hiding place, it was game over.

He began to ease out of her grasp. She snagged his vest.

"Trust me," he whispered in her ear.

A shudder worked its way through her. "Don't go."

"No choice."

He carefully turned and inched toward the opening. Standing there, motionless and barely breathing, he saw a man's shadow pass within inches of their hiding place.

Brady pounced. Tackled him to the ground. They rolled downhill, tussling, each trying to get the upper hand. Where was the gun? He got an elbow to the face. Blood gushed from his nose. Fire burning through his veins, he landed two blows of his own. This guy had hurt Olivia. He was not going to escape.

Feminine voices registered. "Stop! Both of you. Captain, let him go!"

A light beam passed over them. Uniform. Marine cammies.

Brady jumped off him and held up his hands. The flashlight holder, a red-haired female marine, jogged over and, grabbing the other guy's hand, propelled him to his feet. Olivia was two steps behind her.

"Brady, this is Cat," Olivia said. "Corporal Baker. And that is Lance Corporal Franklin."

Corporal Baker nodded a curt greeting and bounced the light between them. "Lance Corporal Franklin, didn't anyone teach you to watch your six?"

"I thought you had my back, Corporal." He cast a wary glance at Brady.

"I would have if you hadn't blazed ahead." Corporal Baker wrinkled her nose in disgust. "Just think if he'd been the enemy." She shifted her gaze to Brady. "I was waiting in my patrol car when I heard the alert about shots fired. Franklin was nearby, and he and I joined the search."

"I apologize for the ambush," Brady said, chest heaving. "I thought you were the shooter. He was here five minutes ago. Did you see him?"

The corporal frowned. "We came in the second entrance. No sign of him." She started up the incline. "We'll give you a ride to the hangar."

"We have to look for him," he countered. "We can't let him leave the base."

"There are others searching for him," she shot over her shoulder. "I have orders to bring you to headquarters, and the one giving them outranks you."

Brady tamped down the tide of frustration. In this career, sometimes orders were in direct opposition to his instincts.

At the patrol car, Brady and Olivia scooted into the back seat. The overhead dome light illuminated the lance corporal's black eye. Brady winced, feeling guilty, then caught a glance of his own bloodied nose in the rearview mirror. The younger marine had given as good as he'd got.

Corporal Baker handed a wad of napkins over the seat. Olivia's eyes were dark with concern as she watched him try to stem the bleeding.

"Your hand will need attention, too," she said.

"Right now the adrenaline rush is distracting me."

"It will fade soon, and then you'll be in pain." Leaning forward, she touched the corporal's shoulder. "Will there be a medic on scene?"

"We'll arrange for one."

"It's a scrape and bloody nose," he said, unaccustomed to anyone caring about his welfare.

Relaxing against the cushion, she took his injured hand and cradled it. "I hate to tell you, but you've got splinters embedded in a gash that will most likely need stitches."

The thrill her tender touch incited wasn't right. In his mind, she belonged to Derek and always would.

He gently disengaged and rested his hand on his thigh. "How's your ankle?"

She clasped her hands together in her lap. "It's sore, but I don't think I did further damage."

"We'll have the medic take a look at it, too."

During the brief trip between the marina and the hangars, they encountered multiple MPs. They were on the hunt. The tables had turned, and the shooter was now the target. He wouldn't take the obvious exit. Most likely, he'd used the river to access the base.

They were ushered inside the hangar and up the stairs, to the offices on the second floor. His CO was the first to meet them. He did not look pleased.

His flinty gaze bounced between Brady and Olivia. "Which one of you is going to tell me exactly what's going on?"

Unable to sit still, Olivia paced the length of the boardroom-style table and nursed a cup of bitter coffee. Her gaze returned repeatedly to Brady's face. He was seated in the end chair closest to the meeting room door. A medic sat on one side of him and was painstakingly picking out the wooden slivers in his palm. His teeth were clenched. His other fist was balled atop his rigid thigh. She didn't like his pallor. Nor did she like that the lieutenant colonel was tearing into him for something that wasn't his fault.

"You should've told me what was going on," George said again, a vein bulging in his temple. "You brought danger to the flight line and every single person in the vicinity."

"No, he didn't."

Both men looked at her in surprise.

"I'm the one who should've told you." Setting her coffee on the table, she said, "Brady is not to blame. The trouble that I'm in has *nothing* to do with him."

George's eyes softened. "I knew something was wrong when I saw the MP with you. But you're mistaken. Whether you want to admit it or not, he is involved. Brady was the target tonight, not you."

Brady's brows tugged together, and his lips clamped closed.

Olivia used a chair for support. In the race for survival, she hadn't stopped to think. The lieutenant colonel might be right. "He couldn't have known I'd be here," she murmured. "It was a last-minute decision. Even if he followed me here, he wouldn't have had time to get into position. Brady, on the other hand…"

His blue-gray eyes were stormy. "Don't blame yourself. You have no control over this guy."

George sighed, the red flush of anger receding. "He must've decided to rid himself of Olivia's protector. With you out of the way, his task would become more achievable."

"He's done his homework," Brady said. "He found out somehow that I would be flying tonight."

"That's not reassuring." George kneaded his temples. "I don't want to believe that anyone on this base would give up sensitive information for a payout."

Brady winced and jerked his hand out of the medic's reach.

"Sorry, sir. The numbing shot I gave you should kick in any minute."

Olivia strode to his side and spoke to the ginger-haired stranger. "Why don't you stop what you're doing and give it time to work?"

He looked undecided until George ordered him to fetch him coffee.

Brady gave her a strained smile. "You didn't have to do that."

"Yes, I did."

The blood had been cleaned from his face, and his nose didn't appear to have been broken. She dearly longed to brush his hair off his forehead, to test the texture of the shining strands. She wished she had the power to drive away his pain and discomfort.

MPs arrived to take their statements. The medic also returned, finished cleaning out Brady's wound and stitched the gash closed. When everyone had left, George told them he was going to order sandwiches and drinks.

"Get comfortable," he ordered. "You won't be free to leave until every acre of this base has been cleared."

The door whooshed closed, leaving them alone in the meeting room. Brady left his chair and walked around to where she was sitting. Swiping a marker from a container of pens, he sank down beside her and gestured to her cast. "May I?"

She settled her arm on the table and watched him print his name. He tapped the fish drawing and smiled. "Nice touch. I would attempt a helicopter, but it wouldn't be recognizable."

When she didn't respond, his smile faded. "What are you thinking about?"

"I hate that you're here with me."

His gaze fell away, and he clutched the marker.

"I hate that you got dragged into this mess," she amended, clearing her throat. "But I'm also glad that it's you and not Derek."

His head shot up. "I don't understand."

"If he were here, he'd be cracking jokes. I couldn't handle that."

"He had a gift for making people forget their problems."

"A good quality."

Brady was watching her closely. "Most of the time," he murmured.

Olivia missed Derek's larger-than-life presence. He'd been the fun guy, determined to live in the moment. He'd also been the master of distraction. But sometimes life required more than jokes. There had been times when she wondered if their relationship would've withstood life's trials.

Olivia felt terrible entertaining such thoughts and hadn't planned to voice them to another person. She shouldn't have said anything, especially to Brady.

"Can I ask you something?"

"About?"

"Derek."

He replaced the marker in its container. "What about him?"

"Did you ever notice his preoccupation with privacy?"

Leaning back in the cushioned chair, he swiveled toward her. "He wasn't interested in social media, I know that much."

"It was more than that." She smoothed her hand along the length of her braid. "He was almost paranoid about keeping a low profile. I never got a clear explanation why he wanted me to keep my maiden name. He said something about his mom keeping hers as a show of independence. We argued about it. As usual, he got his way in the end. I shared one wedding photo online, and he nearly flipped. I thought it was due to his military training, but I'm rethinking that theory."

Brady's expression was difficult to read. "We are taught to be careful in our online activity," he said slowly. "Safety is a priority."

She got the feeling he was being evasive. "He took it to the extreme, though."

"Oh, I nearly forgot." Reaching into her back pocket, she retrieved the folded newspaper. "This was in one of his shirt pockets. I can't imagine why he'd be interested in something like this. I was hoping you could provide some insight."

TEN

The words on the page made no sense. His mind couldn't process the news article's meaning thanks to the spike of apprehension in his system.

No reason to panic, he told himself, scanning the article about a string of violent crimes. There was no mention of the Giordanos. "I'm sorry. I can't help you."

He slid it across the table and prayed she'd drop the subject.

Her brows smashed together. "He didn't mention this town to you?"

"No." Brady kept his face and voice neutral. Inside, he was grateful the town in the article wasn't the same one Derek had resided in. "I've never heard of it."

Why, oh why, had he ever promised to keep this secret? Derek's confession had had the effect of an earthquake, and he was still feeling the aftershocks. His closest friend had been living a lie. He'd created an elaborate ruse, complete with a classic American backstory featuring people who didn't exist and experiences he'd made up. Derek had fed Brady and Olivia the lines, and they'd believed them without question. As Derek's best friend, the deception had been hard to process and even more difficult to forgive. But Olivia was his *wife*. She'd entered a sacred union with the make-believe version of him.

Brady hadn't had long to feel bad for her or to convince Derek to tell her who he really was. He'd passed mere weeks later. Afterward, Brady hadn't even considered telling her. Tarnishing her memories of her dead husband would accomplish nothing.

Decisions he made long ago were now at odds, though. He'd made a promise to stay silent, which meant he was breaking his commitment to honesty. The more he learned of her true character, the more the prospect of hurting her bothered him. Tell her or deceive her? Neither option gave him peace.

Olivia shoved the paper into her pocket. "I'll check the rest of his clothes when I get a chance. Maybe there are more articles that will shed light on why this was important enough to hang on to."

George returned with their supper, and they ate in silence. Marines who'd served with Derek dropped in to check on them. They were glad to see Olivia, of course, but expressed dismay over the circumstances. The office eventually emptied of everyone besides essential personnel. Brady's patience was wearing thin by the time the lieutenant colonel gave them permission to leave.

Corporal Baker drove them to Olivia's house. Another MP was already in the driveway and reported no activity in the vicinity.

"Sergeant Conner has the overnight shift," Cat informed Olivia. "I'll be back tomorrow afternoon."

"Thank you for everything," Olivia said, her voice full of gratitude.

"I didn't do anything besides play chauffeur. The captain here is the true hero."

Olivia blushed. "He is, isn't he?"

"Enough of that," Brady groaned. "Please, tell the lance corporal again how sorry I am for earlier."

"I'll think about it." Cat grinned. "Franklin's a cocky guy and can stand to eat humble pie now and then."

After she left, Brady insisted on doing a sweep of the house. When he was satisfied they didn't have unwanted guests, he pulled off his shoes and stretched out on the couch.

Olivia crossed her arms and stared at him. "Make yourself at home, why don't you?"

"You know I'm not leaving you alone."

"Scared to go home, Captain?"

He hid a smile. "Don't tell anyone."

Sighing, she pulled something from her pocket and eased onto the coffee table. She leaned toward him and extended her hand, palm up.

"I was about to give you this when we were rudely interrupted."

Brady scooted up to rest against the cushioned couch arm. The twin silver disks fell into his outstretched hand with a clink.

His chest seized. "Derek's dog tags."

"He wanted you to have them."

He ran his fingertips over the imprinted words. The name was fake and the social security number probably "borrowed" from a deceased person. But the man who'd earned Brady's respect and friendship had been very real. He missed him every single day.

Lifting his gaze, he found Olivia watching him. "Thank you."

Her smile was wistful. "I told you earlier that I'm glad you're here with me. I can confidently say Derek would be glad, too."

The next morning, Brady insisted on following Olivia to work. The salt-truck delivery driver had to have been new, because he got wedged in the curved access ramp and blocked the employee parking lot. After a fifteen-minute wait, she asked another employee to walk with her inside so that Brady could go on ahead to work. Thankfully, George was aware of their situation and would let his tardiness slide.

As she let herself into her office and perused her emails, her thoughts kept returning to that morning and how Brady's presence should've made things awkward but didn't. After she'd descended the stairs, she'd found his pillow stacked atop a precision-fold blanket. The aroma of roasted coffee had lured her to the kitchen, where he'd greeted her with a smile and a brewed cup waiting for her. They'd taken their coffee and toasted bagels to the table and discussed their respective work agendas. The exchange would've been pleasantly mundane if it hadn't turned to Detective Shaw's investigation and their hope that he'd uncover new information soon.

"Olivia? Do you have a moment?"

Startled, she bumped a container of paper clips and tie tacks off the desk. "Zach." She stared at the dark-headed, bearded man in the doorway. He was wearing his usual flannel shirt, khaki pants and lumberjack boots. "Um, sure, I have time."

Rolling her chair out of the way, she bent to gather the spilled items.

"I didn't mean to interrupt important work," the vet said, joining her beside her desk.

"You didn't. I was reading through some correspondence."

He helped her clean up the mess and, when she was seated again, closed the door. Immediately, her internal alarm jangled. Could the kind-faced vet be hiding a violent streak?

"What's on your mind, Zach?"

He took the chair opposite and propped his arms on the side rests. "I'd like to know why you pointed the cops my direction. I had a visit from a detective late last night who launched very pointed questions at me." His brown eyes brimmed with disappointment. "I'm sorry about your current troubles, Olivia, but how could you possibly think I'm responsible?"

"The police are looking into every person I have contact with here," she hedged. "You aren't being singled out."

His chin jutted. "I didn't get that impression. This wasn't a casual interrogation. He brought officers to search my home, but I told him to get a warrant first."

"If you have nothing to hide—"

"If?" He pounded the desk with his fist. "You do doubt me, then."

Bolting to his feet, he began to pace the tight space. Olivia felt cornered. Trapped. She stood, too, and rolled her chair into its slot. Her pulse raced, slowed, raced again. Zach was a certified diver. He'd know how to sabotage a dive. But was he familiar with carbon monoxide gas? Was he skilled with a sniper rifle?

Zach swerved and stalked behind her desk. She backed up and bumped into the shelving unit.

He stopped short, his frown deepening. "I'd never hurt you, Olivia. I happen to like you. Very much. I want for us to get to know each other better, when you're ready to date again."

"Zach, please—"

"Don't say no. In fact, don't say anything. This isn't the time." He gestured to her cast. "You're obviously under a great deal of strain and aren't thinking clearly."

The door swung open. Maya stood in the hall, her hand

on her hip. "Olivia, Roman sent me to find you. He wants to go over some data or something."

Zach's attempt to mask his displeasure was unsuccessful. "We'll finish this discussion later."

He edged past Maya, his footsteps swallowed up by the carpet.

Olivia didn't move. Relief that Maya had shown up filled her. She had been right to tell Detective Shaw about Zach.

Maya huffed. "Can we go now? Bruno and his buddies are here to see me."

They navigated the corridors and employee elevators in silence. Maya was absorbed by her phone, her fingers skimming over the keyboard as she fired off texts, probably to Bruno, her boyfriend. Near the penguin exhibit, she veered into the restroom. Olivia lingered by the water fountains. While the director's orders that she always be in the company of another staff member wasn't convenient, she couldn't help but be grateful.

The minutes dragged on, and Olivia entered the restroom to check on Maya.

The younger woman stood before the long counter and mirrors. Olivia watched her pop a pill into her mouth and suck in water from the faucet. The prescription container got knocked to the ground in the process. Olivia picked it up and noticed the name printed in black letters.

"Maya, this isn't your prescription."

She snatched the bottle, scratching Olivia's hand with her long nails in the process. "Mind your own business."

When Olivia had first come to work at the aquarium, Maya had been a different person. She'd had an air of innocence, even naivete, about her. That was long gone. Her eyes had a hardened look now, and Olivia blamed the rough crowd she'd fallen in with.

"I'm worried about you."

For a second, Maya's features softened. Then she scowled. "You're not my mom, okay? These aren't serious. They're allergy meds, that's all."

Olivia had seen the label information and knew that she was lying. "I care what happens to you."

"I'm fine."

There was a distinct lack of conviction behind the words. "When I was growing up, my mom advised me to choose friends wisely. Friends who pull me closer to God. Friends who respect me and want good things for me. Can you say that about Bruno?"

Maya blinked fast and averted her face. "Bruno loves me. His crew accepts me. That's all I need."

Tamping down a sigh, Olivia followed her onto the landing and noticed a knot of young men pushing and shoving one another. They were laughing and using off-color language. Thankfully, there weren't other guests nearby to overhear. The burliest one extracted himself and loped over to Maya. He seized her by the back of the neck and crushed his lips to hers. She seemed to wilt in his arms, as if she was afraid to protest.

Olivia recognized the tattoo on his neck. The local papers had run a story about a street gang and had mentioned the distinguishable mark. While Bruno and Maya were occupied, the others turned their collective attention to her. Their eyes bore evidence of a harsh existence. One with lank brown hair and scruffy facial hair ogled her. He whispered something to another man, something that elicited a bark of laughter. Then he headed her direction, his mouth shifting into a leer. Unease skittered down her spine.

The director's appearance halted his approach. Ruth's

shrewd gaze took in the scene and landed on Maya. "I assume your friends can all produce admission tickets?"

Maya shrugged off Bruno's arm. Her face flamed. "They aren't here to see the exhibits. They only came inside for a few minutes."

"Send them on their way. After that, come to my office."

"Yes, ma'am."

Bruno shot Ruth a baleful look before motioning for the others to follow him. Ruth came to stand beside Olivia while the group shuffled out a side entrance.

The smartly dressed brunette eventually turned to her. "I saw a news article about a shooting on the air station. You still live there, correct?"

Her stomach sank. Would the director bar her from working? "For nine more days."

"The article didn't mention names of those involved, but I have to ask. Does it have to do with the recent attacks?"

She nodded. "Someone shot at the captain and me. The military police are coordinating with Jacksonville PD to find the shooter."

"I see." Her expression turned sympathetic. "I'm not certain it's in your best interest to continue working." Waving toward the glass wall, she said, "While we have extra security on hand, I can't guarantee your safety."

"What do you expect me to do? Sit inside my apartment until this guy is caught? That could take weeks. Months." He could evade the law entirely. A depressing, frightening thought. "I have bills to pay. More importantly, I don't want to lose this job. Please, Ruth."

Mouth pinched, Ruth stared into the distance. Olivia held her breath. Without her work, how would she keep from obsessing over her faceless enemy?

"I understand what you're going through," she said at last. "My sister encountered some trouble last year. Threatening notes. Break-ins. The guy played mind games with her, toying with her like a cat does a mouse. She said her work was the only thing that kept her going."

"Is she all right?"

"Yes, she's fine. They identified the guy, and he's behind bars."

"I'm glad."

The skin above Ruth's nose crinkled. "I'll let you stay, as long as you promise to be on your guard at all times."

Olivia restrained herself from giving her a hug. "Thank you."

"Don't thank me. I'm not entirely sure this is the right decision."

"I'll be careful."

"You're set to speak at the gala this weekend?"

"Yes." The gala was being held in the River Expedition building, and she was part of the staff responsible for setting up the tables and decorating.

"Perhaps having you front and center isn't such a good idea. Would Roman be able to take your place?"

Olivia searched for the right words. She didn't want to downplay his role or discount his value.

"Never mind. Your reservations are obvious."

"I planned out the speech and committed it to memory. It wouldn't be fair to ask him to step in at the last minute."

Ruth audibly exhaled. "I was planning on hiring extra security, anyway. We'll be vigilant to check everyone's credentials and belongings."

Olivia relaxed. She'd worked hard on her presentation and had been looking forward to this event for months.

"Ruth?"

They both turned to see the gift shop manager hurrying past a pair of moms pushing strollers.

"Is there a problem?"

"You know the overdue shipment of stuffed animals we received last night? They've been stolen."

Ruth frowned. "Are you sure they haven't been misplaced?"

"I'm positive. Hank and I have searched both buildings."

"Excuse me, Olivia." Glancing out the glass wall, Ruth pointed to Maya, who was still chatting with Bruno. "Wait on your escort."

Olivia nodded, her thoughts caught on the upcoming gala. It was a black-tie event, complete with a live band and buffet catered by a popular waterfront restaurant. Last year, she'd gone alone because Derek had been on a training mission. She'd assumed she'd be going alone again this year. Brady was determined to be with her during their nonworking hours. Would he be her date? The idea released a flurry of butterflies in her stomach.

She'd rushed into a relationship with Derek, thanks to the heady effect of his full-on pursuit and innate charm. It wasn't until after the wedding that she'd realized how little she knew about him. That couldn't happen again.

She rubbed the empty space on her finger where her wedding rings used to be. *Be sensible, Olivia. Brady is the last person you should be interested in. He will never see you as anything more than his best friend's wife.*

ELEVEN

"Do you have a tuxedo?"

Baffled by the abrupt greeting, Brady walked past her and stopped in the middle of her living room. "Hello, Olivia. How was your day? No trouble at work, I guess."

She closed the door and gave him an arch look. "You know the answer to those questions, seeing as the last text you sent me was—" holding up one finger, she checked her phone "—thirty-five minutes ago. I received one an hour before that and another during lunch. Shall I go on?"

"I did warn you about that." If he couldn't be with her, he needed to know she was okay.

"Well? Do you?"

"I do not own a tuxedo. In fact, I don't know anyone who has one in their closet."

"Can you rent one on short notice?"

"For?"

"The gala is this Sunday night. I can't miss it."

"I'll locate one."

She worried her lower lip. "You're sure you don't mind? The place is going to be crawling with security. This guy would have to be insane to attempt anything."

"We haven't ruled that out." He caught a whiff of herbs and garlic, and his stomach growled. "Did you cook?"

A self-conscious expression played over her face. "I left a few pots and pans unpacked." He followed her to the kitchen. "I defrosted a package of chicken and sautéed it with vegetables. Nothing fancy."

"Fancy? I grew up on bologna and cheese sandwiches. I don't know the meaning of the word." He snagged a small cube of chicken and popped it into his mouth. He made an appreciative sound. "Is it ready now?"

She smiled, and her eyes glowed with pleasure. "It's nice to cook for someone again. Cooking for one person isn't fun."

"You can cook for me anytime," he said, his voice husky.

Neither one moved. Brady's gaze roamed her face, snagging on her coral-tinted lips. What would she do if he lowered his head and kissed her?

He blinked and forced his focus elsewhere. This was wrong. They were standing in the home she'd shared with Derek. He felt like a traitor.

"I'll, uh, get the plates and forks."

There was a telltale blush on her cheeks. He told himself he was imagining things. She couldn't be attracted to him. Shouldn't be interested in anything more than friendship. Because he was damaged, and even worse, he was keeping a major secret from her.

When they were seated and she'd prayed over the meal, Brady steered the conversation to innocent topics. He peppered her about her childhood in the western part of the state. After answering a dozen questions, she blushed and apologized for monopolizing the conversation.

"Nothing about you bores me," he reassured her.

She met his gaze head-on, and the push-pull of need and want was there again. Her hand was right there, inches from his own. Her nails were coated with a sheer gloss. A thin bracelet encircled her wrist. His fingers itched to trace the gold, to explore the contours of her delicate bone structure. He removed his hands from the table and settled them on his lap, away from temptation.

He'd been alone for too long. Sure, he went out on dates occasionally. His hang-ups prevented any serious connections from forming, however.

The doorbell trilled, and Olivia went to answer the summons. He was a couple of steps behind. The MP on duty informed her that Detective Shaw wanted to see her. When she approved the visit, Shaw left his personal vehicle, traversed the sidewalk and entered the house.

"They're being thorough," he said. "I approve."

Brady was apprehensive about her upcoming change of address. "We have to identify this guy, Shaw. After next weekend, she'll be in a civilian setting without the benefit of armed marines. Do you have any leads?"

He waved a folder. "I do, in fact."

Shaw perched on the recliner's edge, and she and Brady sat side by side on the couch.

"We did some digging into the aquarium vet, Dr. Zach Ledford, and we learned that he did a stint in the army. Get this—he was a sniper."

Olivia sucked in an audible breath. "He paid me a visit today."

"What?" Brady angled toward her. "You didn't mention that in your texts."

"He was upset about being a suspect. He said he denied the police access to his home."

Shaw nodded. "We're waiting on a warrant. In the meantime, he has the opportunity to hide or destroy evidence."

"As an aquarium employee," Olivia said, "he has complete access and knowledge of the layout. But does he have a way onto the base?"

"Because he's not retired—medically or otherwise—

he doesn't have a military ID. That means no access to the base."

"Unless he falsified one," Brady muttered, thinking of Derek. All one had to have these days is the right criminal connections.

Shaw's gray brows lifted. "True. Or he could've befriended a military member in order to gain a visitor pass. We're working with PMO on that front. They're supposed to review the pass records for the days leading up to the shooting. Another strike against him? He doesn't have a confirmable alibi. He says he left the aquarium at three o'clock and went straight home, where he remained alone all night."

"He doesn't work regular hours at the aquarium," Olivia said. "He comes in at odd times."

Brady touched Olivia's cast. "It's not safe for you to work around him."

Her chin assumed a stubborn tilt. "I've already had this conversation with the director. I'm not quitting."

"You don't have to quit. Take a leave of absence."

"We don't know for certain that Zach is the culprit," she argued. "I know the evidence points to him, but I have serious doubts."

"Because he looks like a regular guy? Because he's a respected veterinarian?"

"Because I trust my instincts."

Shaw cleared his throat, drawing their attention back to him. "Anyway, going into hiding may make it more difficult to snag him."

Brady's temper flared. "Are you suggesting using Olivia as bait?"

"If she continues her duties as usual, with safeguards in place, he won't have cause to panic and bolt. He'll assume he's in the clear. All the while, we'll be building our case."

"And when he attempts to kill her again?"

Her cool fingers rested on his arm. "Whoever is behind the attacks won't get the chance. I'll have at least one other staff member with me at all times."

Brady covered her hand and held fast. "I don't like this."

"Brady, I'm not going to take any undue risks. I promise."

Snared in her molten gaze, Brady tried to pinpoint the exact moment Olivia had gotten to him. Somehow, she'd become more than a perceived duty. Her happiness and safety were linked to his peace of mind. The knowledge frightened him. He'd rather be piloting a helo with scant fuel and no place to land than to risk pain like his parents had inflicted. In his world, trust was foolish and love the ultimate sin.

Loneliness had made his heart reckless. If he wasn't careful, he'd wind up confused and alone like the pitiful little boy he'd once been, glued to the windows day after day. Waiting, hoping, praying the beat-up gold station wagon would turn into the gravel drive.

He speared Shaw with a glance. "Work quickly, Detective."

"I despise functions like this," Roman muttered, snapping the brushed silver tablecloth in midair and watching it float into place on the round table. "Why can't we just do our jobs instead of wasting time schmoozing with industry professionals?"

Olivia hid a smile as she smoothed the air bubbles beneath the textured cloth. Her gruff, burly assistant looked out of place amid the posh scene being staged for the gala. The meeting space was large enough to accommodate approximately two hundred people. Floor-to-ceiling windows along two walls provided stunning views of the river, the bridge spanning it and the businesses hugging the opposite side. An aquarium exhibit was housed on the third side of the room, and a raised platform along the interior would host the band and speakers. A circular space in the middle of the tables would be reserved for dancing. Right now the large room was a hive of activity, as aquarium staff arranged tables and chairs and set up the buffet equipment. In two days' time, it would be transformed into an elegant oasis alive with music and conversation.

Surely her enemy wouldn't try to strike then.

She hefted an oversize glass vase onto the table. "These events can actually be a lot of fun." When he rolled his eyes, she said, "You enjoy good food, don't you?"

"In my experience, meals prepared in mass quantities are substandard at best." He nudged his glasses farther up his nose. "I'm going to stay long enough to hear your presentation, then I'm gone."

"You should be on the stage with me," she said. "I know you're not a fan of public speaking, but your project input could at least be acknowledged. I can introduce you and let the people applaud your accomplishments. You wouldn't have to say anything."

He scrubbed one hand over his beard. "Not happening."

"Why not?"

"Third grade."

"What happened in third grade?"

"I was cast as Charlie Brown in a Peanuts play. I forgot my lines. The other kids laughed. Mortified, I froze. Then I fled."

Olivia winced. "Harsh."

"I've avoided the spotlight ever since." He gestured over his shoulder. "I'll get more chairs."

She would've moved on to the next table, but the box

containing the tablecloths was empty. The person in charge of the setup, events coordinator Wanda McLemore, told Olivia where to find more.

"Is there someone who can go and get them?"

The aquarium was closed, and Olivia preferred to remain within the hub of activity. Recalling Brady's intensity last night, the turbulence in his blue-gray eyes, she had no desire to venture off alone. In fact, she'd promised him she wouldn't.

The flustered coordinator had no patience for her request. "Why can't you do it? As you can see, everyone is busy pitching in." Her tone accused Olivia of being lazy.

"I'll go with you."

Olivia turned around, not surprised at Maya's offer. It would get her out of her current task—tying silver ribbons to the chairs.

"Hurry up." Wanda slipped a shallow pan into the serving slot and wiped her damp forehead with her sleeve. "We have loads to do between now and Sunday."

They left the hustle and bustle behind. The deserted, darkened hallways put Olivia on instant alert. Maya had already whipped out her phone and was texting someone.

"Do you have a dress for Sunday?" Olivia ventured, missing their former camaraderie.

"I'm not going."

They were passing through the turtle exhibit, lit by the tanks' soft glow. "Why not?"

"Bruno doesn't want me to. He's not happy that I got reprimanded for having visitors."

Olivia didn't bother pointing out Maya had violated the rules by letting her friends in for free. "Do *you* want to attend?"

She tucked her phone into her back pocket and ran her fingers along the tank glass. "I don't care."

Seemed Maya didn't care about much anymore besides pleasing her boyfriend. Inside the industrial-size kitchen, she flipped on the overhead lights. "You used to love your work."

"Yeah, I did." Bristling, she glared at Olivia. "That was before I figured out I couldn't trust my coworkers."

She paused beside the stoves. "What are you implying?"

Leaning close, she poked Olivia's shoulder. "You told Ruth about the prescription pills, didn't you? I saw you chatting her up while I was outside with my friends."

Their isolation wasn't lost on Olivia. Apprehension rushed to the surface before she dismissed it. This was Maya. Her surly attitude didn't mean she was capable of murder.

"I didn't speak to Ruth about you. It must've been someone else."

"You're lying."

"Believe what you want."

"She threatened to fire me, you know. Not because of Bruno and his friends, but because someone claimed I'm using. I explained it was a misunderstanding."

"Was it, though? I saw the label. Those weren't allergy pills. Did Bruno give them to you?"

Maya sneered. "You don't know what you're talking about."

"You're clearly in over your head with these guys. I'd like to help you, if I can."

"I don't need your help."

Maya's phone jangled. She edged to the far side of the room and started a hushed conversation. With a sigh, Olivia rounded the fridge and entered the area housing decorating supplies. There was no door, to her relief. Memories of being locked in the basement storage were too fresh.

While she searched for the right color tablecloths, she prayed for her young coworker. Nothing good would come from her association with a gang.

It took several minutes of searching to locate the silver ones. She lugged three boxes, one by one, into the kitchen and placed them on the prep table. "Maya, will you carry one of the boxes?"

The sudden silence held sinister expectation.

Hard knots formed in her midsection. "Maya? You still in here?"

Trying to remain calm, she rushed to the door through which they'd entered and peered into the hallway. She couldn't hear or see the other woman. Frustration warred with fear.

Maya knew Olivia wasn't supposed to be alone, but she'd been angry. Had she left out of spite? Been called away to an emergency? Or had the man after Olivia wanted Maya out of the way?

The lights flickered out, submerging the space in inky black shadows.

Her heart slammed against her rib cage. Fumbling for her phone, she used the flashlight feature as a guide.

People. She needed the safety of people.

She had to reach the others, before—

No. Don't think like that.

This was a temporary power outage. The generators would kick in any second.

As she retraced her steps, Olivia imagined hot breath on her neck again. Or was it real? The hair on her nape stood to attention, and a prickly sensation stole over her scalp.

Breaking into a run, she'd reached the exhibits when her foot connected with something solid. She threw her hands up to brace her fall and collided with a water fountain mounted to the wall. Her phone was jarred from her fingers and landed on the carpet facedown, obliterating the light.

Olivia pushed upright and squinted at the space around her feet.

The blow came out of nowhere. Her head whipped to the right.

Pain radiated through her cheek and eye socket and snaked down her neck.

Knocked off balance, she fell onto her knees. A hand bunched in her hair and jerked her backward before she could crawl out of reach. She filled her lungs with air and screamed with all her might.

Her attacker released his hold on her hair and, looming over her, wrapped his gloved fingers around her throat and squeezed. She kicked out and landed a solid hit to his inner thigh. He grunted and increased the pressure. Tears leaked from the corners of her eyes.

Need air now.

She used both hands to try to peel his fingers away.

He was too strong. Relentless. In the dark, she could make out the whites of his eyes through the mask holes.

This can't be the end, Lord.

But she couldn't draw breath. Her lungs were going to explode.

Dots danced on the back of her eyelids.

The strength slowly leached from her body, until she couldn't fight anymore.

TWELVE

She was being dragged through the aquarium by her feet. Struggling to shake off the confusing haze, Olivia attempted to get her bearings and saw the restrooms from an unexpected angle. Carpet chafed her skin. Pain was not her friend. Or maybe that's what had jarred her from unconsciousness.

The exit sign up ahead kicked her brain into high gear. That door led to the parking lot and an unknown end.

The generators had come on, but their limited power was meant for animal support, not unnecessary output like overhead lighting. She couldn't make out any defining details about the man with the iron grip on her ankles.

Help me, Lord, please. I can't escape on my own. I need You.

Olivia concentrated on keeping her limbs loose and fluid. Sudden tension would alert him to the fact she was capable of fighting back. Carefully scanning the passing surroundings, her gaze lit on a fire extinguisher. The makeshift weapon was housed in a glass-fronted box. She'd have to break it.

Mustering her courage, she twisted her entire body and managed to kick free. His grunt of surprise morphed into an enraged growl. She clambered onto her knees and found her footing. Lunging for the fire extinguisher, she brought her cast down hard, shattering the glass. Before she could grasp the extinguisher, his arms wrapped around her middle like heavy chains. He jerked hard, digging into her diaphragm and wrenching her around.

Her back to him, she elbowed him in the gut. Ground her heel into his toes. Used her cast to hammer at his relentless grip. Desperation lent her an edge. She couldn't let him get the upper hand. Couldn't lose consciousness again.

Olivia continued the onslaught until his hold faltered. Breaking free, she ripped the extinguisher from its box and whirled around, hitting him as hard as she could. It hit him in the soft flesh of his neck and was enough to momentarily stun him.

She had no time to plan her escape, to examine which route was best.

She sprinted past the restrooms. She had to reach the others. If she could get close enough for them to hear her cries for help—

His fingers clawed down her back, grasping at the fabric of her shirt. She screamed. Pumped her legs harder. Faster.

The hallway split, and she took a sharp right. A cleaning cart was parked against the wall. Olivia shoved it behind her and tipped it over, spilling the contents and buying herself precious seconds. The shadows worked in her favor. She heard him tumble into the wall.

But her momentary victory didn't last. She didn't see the bucket until it was too late. Her sprained ankle landed inside the shallow pail at an awkward angle, and she sprawled onto the carpet facedown. His footsteps spelled her doom. If he caught her again, he'd make sure she didn't wake up.

Horror a metallic taste in her mouth, she crawled into the nearest room and prayed he hadn't seen which direction she'd taken. A sliver of light from an outside source revealed she was in the kitchen again. She hurried past the stoves, backtracked and grabbed a knife from the butcher block, then limped past the fridge and into the storage space.

Olivia crouched in the darkened corner, the knife handle clutched in her palm. Her frantic heartbeat crowded out all sounds. She wouldn't hear his approach. Did he have a gun on him?

Amid the chaos of her thoughts, there was one constant. Brady.

She didn't want to leave him like this. He'd blame himself. He'd sink further into protective solitude. He'd be alone forever. That would be a tragedy.

Above the sound of her bated breath, she heard someone's stealthy approach. She clamped her lips together to trap a terrified wail.

Their shoes squeaked against the tile. Slow. Unsure. Or methodical? Thorough? Which was it?

The fridge hummed to life. The power surged back on. Seconds later, light flooded the room. Not good.

A face peeked around the corner, and Olivia raised the knife.

"Olivia? What are you doing?"

"Maya!" she hissed. Surging upright, she held tight to the knife. "He's down here. Did you see him?"

"Who?" She stepped more fully into the space, her gaze wary. "What happened to your face? Why are you bleeding?" She pointed to the myriad small cuts on her hand.

"My attacker. He's here."

"I didn't see anyone."

"Can I use your phone? I lost mine. We need to notify security and the local police."

Maya watched with wide, frightened eyes as Olivia rattled off explanations into the phone. She was still speaking to Jacksonville PD when the head of security marched in.

Don Welch expressed concern over her ordeal and utter confidence they would locate this guy. He got on his radio and ordered the night guard to keep a sharp eye on the security cameras, just in case the perp was still in the building.

"I'm really sorry, Olivia. I shouldn't have left you."

"Where did you go?"

"I had a phone call. Bruno was in the parking lot with takeout from my favorite restaurant. I was only gone a few minutes," she said defensively.

"A few minutes was all it took," Olivia told her, hopeful she could keep her emotions in check until she was alone. "He almost got me outside, where he probably had a getaway car waiting."

"You're still here, though," she said, her voice high and thin. "You're fine."

Maya didn't seem to care that she'd almost been abducted. No doubt she was worried her latest mistake would get her fired.

The door swooshed open, and they all tensed. Don reached for his weapon.

"Olivia? You in here?"

At the sound of Brady's voice, her hold on her emotions stretched to the breaking point. She left the storage area and saw him standing by the stoves. The play of confusion, horror and sorrow over his handsome features made her want to weep.

He held out his arms, and she went willingly into them.

"Oh, Liv."

He lifted his hand slowly toward her face and the swollen, angry red welt marring her cheek. She flinched away from his touch. He fisted his hand.

Fury funneled through him to the point he shook with it.

"He got to you, didn't he?" he uttered in a low, controlled voice. "Despite the precautions."

Her lips were devoid of color, and her eyes were caverns of hopelessness. "I don't want to talk about it."

Brady tamped down the questions and reined in the need for retribution. Olivia needed comfort. Right now she needed a friend, not a protector bent on punishing the slug who'd hurt her.

He belatedly noticed Maya and Don Welch. Shame cloaked Maya as she trudged out of the kitchen, her gaze averted. Don told them he'd be out in the hallway standing guard.

Olivia snuggled close, her head tucked beneath his chin and her hand splayed over his heart. He trailed his fingers through her hair. They didn't speak for a long time. When Brady finished running various scenarios through his mind, he turned to prayer. He thanked God for delivering her from the enemy and asked for divine comfort for her. This sort of trial, on top of everything else she'd had to deal with this past year, would cripple a weaker person. But Olivia was strong and resourceful. More important, she was a woman of devout faith.

Little by little, the tension ebbed from her body and a soft sigh escaped her lips, tickling the dip at the base of his throat. Brady continued to stroke her unbound hair, tenderness for this woman welling up inside. He liked that she'd turned to him for solace. He liked that she trusted him with her vulnerability. He liked her, period.

Brady suspected he was in more danger from his own lonely heart than their enemy.

Olivia eased out of his arms. The story spilled out in bursts. Her terror was evident, but so was her bravery.

"I'm incredibly proud of you," he told her.

Tipping her chin toward him, he blinked down into

her huge brown eyes and discovered a hundred mysteries there. What was she thinking? Did she wish he'd give her space? Or close the inches separating them?

Brady's gaze snagged on her cheek. Lowering his head, he brushed the lightest of kisses to the bruised flesh. Her breathing pattern changed. He closed his eyes and forced himself to remember his best friend. Derek—and the secret he'd bequeathed to Brady—stood between them.

With herculean effort, he stepped back. "I'll drive you to the hospital."

"I'm fine."

"Ruth will insist. Besides, you may have reinjured your arm using it as a sledgehammer to reach the fire extinguisher."

She reluctantly agreed. Shaw arrived while she was being examined and waited with Brady in order to take her statement. While he was there, Ruth phoned. Judging by Olivia's expression, it wasn't a pleasant conversation.

"What did she say?" Brady asked.

"We agreed that after the gala, I won't be returning until the case is resolved. I'm allowed to join the upcoming field excursion, but that's it."

"I'm sorry. I know that's not the outcome you wanted."

"It's for the best," she said, trying to be positive. "This way, I can focus all of my energy on the big move."

Brady masked his relief. Staying away from the aquarium wouldn't make her happy, it would lessen the danger.

"I'll be on hand to help you with that. For now, let's focus on the gala and getting through it with no more incidents."

THIRTEEN

Stationed near the platform, Brady reached out and clasped Olivia's hand, stalling the pen's incessant clicking. "You're going to do great," he murmured. She'd rehearsed her speech so many times she could probably recite it in her sleep. "If our guy is here, he won't be able to make a move."

The aquarium director had come through with her promise of heightened security. No one inside this room had escaped a thorough inspection. Shaw had also provided half a dozen plainclothes officers.

Lifting a hand to the sparkly accessory pinning her soft waves into place, she shifted toward him. Her aquamarine dress shimmered in the candlelight. "I'm afraid they'll be wondering how I got this shiner instead of listening to the information being presented."

Unable to resist, he took her chin between his thumb and finger and tipped her face up. Her kohl-rimmed eyes were large and alluring. "Liv, they'd have trouble paying attention no matter what. You're stunning."

She blinked. "I had no idea you were such a charmer, Captain Johnson."

"It's not flattery if it's the truth."

"Olivia." Ruth tapped her on the shoulder. "It's almost time."

Brady lowered his hand, realizing the musicians had finished their set, and those guests not already at the round tables were heading to their seats.

She squared her shoulders and, with a final glance at him, followed the director to the podium. Ruth introduced her. Olivia waited for the polite applause to taper off before asking Roman to stand and be acknowledged. A little way into her speech, a late arrival caused her to falter. Brady stiffened at the sight of Dr. Zach Ledford, whom he recognized from social media photographs Shaw had shown him. The vet found a seat mere steps from the podium, in Olivia's clear line of sight, and directed his full attention to her. She pinched her lips closed and looked down at her notes.

Brady fought the urge to physically remove Ledford. He asked God to grant her courage and renewed focus. Seconds ticked by. Gripping the podium edge, she picked up where she'd left off.

His fists slowly unclenching, he scrutinized Ledford. The vet sat slightly forward in his chair, his gaze riveted on Olivia. Shaw's warrant request had come through, but the officers hadn't found incriminating evidence in his home. Not a surprise, considering he'd been forewarned. They were still waiting to hear if the air station's visitor pass log presented any clues.

When Olivia finished her speech, Brady escorted her to their table near the buffet stations. "Mission successful," he told her. "You were informative, direct and not the least bit boring."

She chuckled. "Thanks, I think."

Once in their seats, Erin flashed a supportive smile and whispered something in her ear. The look she gave Brady was less friendly.

Ruth introduced another speaker. Brady lost his focus as he observed the sea of faces. Was anyone paying particular attention to Olivia? The pool of suspects seemed to widen before his eyes. Their perp could be someone from another aquarium or in a different facet of the industry entirely. He ran a finger beneath this itchy collar as frustration built.

The speaker gave his closing remarks, and the musicians started into a lively tune. Couples migrated to the dance floor.

Spying the wistfulness in Olivia's gaze, he asked her to dance. She was grace and allure, mystery and beauty in one package. He was a fool to think for one second that he'd be good enough for her.

"May I cut in?"

Olivia, who'd at some point linked her arms around his neck, straightened suddenly. Her hands slid down to brace against Brady's chest.

Brady glared at Zach. "No, you may not."

"I wasn't asking your permission." His gaze switched to Olivia. "It's her choice."

Their exchange was drawing the attention of nearby couples.

"I'd rather not, Zach," Olivia said.

He shot Brady a disgruntled look. "May I at least have five minutes of your time? Over at the drink table? Your bodyguard can keep a watchful eye on us the entire time."

"Five minutes," she reluctantly agreed.

Brady inserted himself between them as they walked in a line through the crowd. He stationed himself beside the punch bowl, close enough to evaluate Dr. Ledford's every expression. If he so much as blinked the wrong way, he'd be facedown on the carpet within seconds.

The cloak of contentment she'd experienced in Brady's embrace dissipated. She wasn't at ease around Zach anymore, and he sensed it.

"Relax, Olivia," Zach said. "Your detective didn't find

anything. There was nothing to find because I would never hurt you."

She wanted to believe him. The earnestness in his eyes seemed genuine. "I won't be able to relax until my enemy is in custody."

In a bid to boost her spirits, Brady had taken her in his Cessna to a tiny South Carolina beach town yesterday. They'd spent hours on the secluded beach, walking along the shoreline and collecting seashells. The outing had proved somewhat therapeutic. Brady had opened up to her, treated her as a trusted confidant. She craved more… more time, more insight, a deeper connection.

Zach's gaze seemed to miss nothing. His mouth pulled into a frown. "Who is that man to you? I thought you weren't ready to date."

Answering that question wasn't as easy as it used to be. "Captain Johnson is a close friend."

He glanced at Brady, who hovered a few feet away, his hackles clearly raised. "I get the feeling he views your relationship in a different light."

Butterflies dipped and danced inside at the thought. "You never mentioned you'd served in the army."

"The topic never came up. I didn't deliberately hide the information, and I wasn't the one who took shots at you." He studied her wounded cheek. "I want to protect you, if you'll let me. I can do a better job than that marine is doing."

Ire flared inside her. "Brady has put his life on the line for me, time and again. I wouldn't want anyone else at my side."

"You may live to regret that choice."

FOURTEEN

Olivia and Brady exited the aquarium in the presence of Shaw and the other officers. More than half of the guests had already left. Olivia had mixed feelings—relief there hadn't been any trouble and her speech had sparked interest in the breeding program, but also uncertainty over what lay ahead for her professionally. She had no idea when or even if she'd be permitted to return.

She turned at the sound of her colleague Erin calling her name. Brady reluctantly stepped back, granting them privacy.

"Are you sure you don't want to stay at my place tonight?" This was Erin's second attempt to convince her. "You could do with a change of scenery. And different company."

"I'm positive. I appreciate the offer, though."

Hooking her arm through Olivia's, Erin angled her away from Brady and the other men. Cars maneuvered the parking area on this side of the building. Cold air snuck beneath her full skirt, and she shivered.

"I got the impression you two didn't get along."

"That's no longer the case."

Erin didn't look convinced. "I know how tough this year has been for you, that's all."

She lowered her voice. "Trust me when I say he's been good for me."

"If you change your mind, you have my number."

Olivia nodded. "I'll see you soon."

"Oh right, the field excursion."

The gunning of a car's engine echoed through the night. Brady closed the distance between them. "We shouldn't be out in the open like this."

"I'll check in with you tomorrow," Erin assured her.

An officer walked with them to Brady's truck. Once they were inside the cab, he got into his unmarked vehicle. He'd follow them to the air station, where an MP would be waiting to take over. In six more days, she'd no longer have marines guarding her home.

Brady adjusted the heating vents as he turned onto the main road. She rested her head against the seat and watched the lights from passing businesses stream through the windshield.

"What are you thinking about?" Brady asked.

"How grateful I am that no one got hurt tonight."

"The presence of law enforcement was a deterrent."

She shifted her head in order to study his profile. "Are you hungry? Because I was too keyed up to eat."

"I noticed. We'll make a quick stop at the commissary." He shook his head in mock despair. "Your place is sadly lacking in the ice cream department."

"I told you, that won't be the case at my new place. No sense in stocking up on groceries, only to have to move them in a few days."

"I'll hold you to it."

She glanced in the rearview mirror. "It's nice to have an escort."

"Shaw and the others have gone above and beyond. I can say the same for the MPs."

"Jehovah-jireh."

"What's that? Hebrew?"

"Yes. It means God provides. I've been studying the

different names of God. That one in particular has become meaningful this past year. He's provided for my emotional and material needs." Her eyes grew moist. "And now He's provided you."

He looked startled. "Me?"

"Yes, you. God knew I'd need a friend and protector."

Brady turned contemplative, as if being someone's answer to prayer was a novel idea.

The air station gate came into view, and the officer slowed as Brady executed the right turn. He waved and continued on his way to police headquarters. They pulled in to the visitor area in order to connect with their military escort. Olivia had hoped it would be Corporal Baker, but it was someone new. Lance Corporal Pickens's bloodshot eyes and clenched jaw were at odds with his baby-faced look.

Pickens trailed them to the commissary and parked beside their truck. He had little to say as he walked them to the sliding entrance doors.

"I'll wait here."

Brady nodded. "We won't be long."

Inside the brightly lit store, they breezed through the produce and deli sections. Olivia pointed to the sign above the water fountain. "I'm going to duck into the restroom."

"I'll wait right here." In his pristine black tuxedo, he looked as if he'd stepped out of a James Bond movie. Cool as ice, movie-star handsome and treacherous to a girl's heart.

She was washing her hands when the lights cut off. The darkness was complete. She couldn't see her own hand in front of her face.

The fear was instantaneous. *Not again.*

Olivia used her phone light to see her way past the

blow-dryers and employee lockers, around the corner and through the passage to the door. The spot where Brady had been standing was vacant.

"Brady?"

When she didn't get a response, she knew something was wrong. He wouldn't have left her for no reason. She could hear employees talking in surprised voices. They weren't frightened, like her. They weren't aware of the danger.

She turned off the light. Her enemy had the capability to access sophisticated weaponry. If he was staging an attack, he might be equipped with night vision goggles. He'd see her, but she wouldn't see him. He could stalk her, as a predatory animal would do.

Reaching out in the dark, she located the coupon and magazine stand and crouched behind it. Minutes dragged. Doors slammed. The clang and thud of what was likely aluminum cans reverberated through the aisles.

Alarm slid through her when Brady didn't return. She debated whether or not to text him. The screen light would expose her hiding place.

Had Lance Corporal Pickens realized what was happening? Or was he oblivious to the potential threat?

A commotion in the opposite side of the store incited panic. Someone screamed. The sounds of a scuffle were undeniable. A would-be thief trying to take advantage of the situation? Or her adversary on the hunt?

Olivia fired off a text. She squeezed the phone in her tight grip, her eyes glued to the screen.

He didn't respond.

She had to act. Had to investigate.

With her flashlight feature lighting the way, she used the stand to pull herself up and forced one foot in front of the other. The blood thundered in her ears. Her muscles were coiled like wire springs. She didn't have a weapon, but her cast was hard enough to break someone's nose.

Olivia continued along the back of the store where the meat was stocked. This area had gone as silent as a tomb.

The flashlight beam bounced off white flecked tiles. At each aisle's endcap, she stopped and peeked along the row. A mother and son were seated beside the cereal display. When her light fell on them, they huddled closer together. Maybe they'd sensed this wasn't an ordinary power outage. There were no storms in the area, after all, and they had to have heard the same scuffle she had.

Her mouth sandpaper dry, she tiptoed forward. The next two aisles were empty. Then she saw something that made her stomach swoop to her toes. Blood. Bright red beads, one after another.

She followed the grisly trail, past the cheese and yogurt selections and the refrigerated dairy cases. The beads had become smears and partial footprints. Hardly able to breathe, she rounded the cases and spied a silver door. Her gaze locked on a bloody handprint.

Olivia's instincts told her not to go through the door. But Brady could be on the other side, in desperate need of help.

She inched forward and pushed the swinging door inward. The hinges whined. Clay red tiles hindered her ability to see blood spatters. There were prep tables and rows of razor-sharp knives of increasing size hanging on the wall above deep sinks.

The silence was thick and cloying. Was her enemy biding his time, waiting for the right moment to shoot her? Tackle her? Strangle her?

In the next instant, she sensed someone behind her.

Before she could defend herself, a hand clapped over her mouth and an arm imprisoned her waist.

Olivia was being hauled into the cooler, and her struggles proved futile.

"Shh." Brady pressed his lips to her ear. "It's me."

Olivia's thrashing didn't immediately subside. Her back tucked against his chest; he held fast. "Liv, stop."

Inhaling sharply, she spun out of his hold. "Brady? Are you okay? I saw blood—" Her light scanned his length, from his feet up, stopping on his face. "You're injured!"

"I'm fine. He got me with a knife, but it's not serious." The wound on the side of his neck burned like a scorpion sting. "I'll deal with it later."

"It looks deep. There was a lot of blood. Was he injured, too?"

"No, I don't think so." Putting himself between her and the door, he said, "He ambushed me. I fought him off and pursued him back here but lost sight of him. He could still be in the building."

"He won't stick around and risk being caught. He'll return to the shadows and regroup. Once again, he managed to slip in and out without leaving a clue to his identity."

"On that point, you're wrong." Fishing the object from his pocket, he lifted it for her to see. "He left us a souvenir."

"The knife he used on you." She grimaced, her gaze going again to his wound. "You're not feeling light-headed, are you?"

"Not at all."

At the sound of approaching footsteps, he lifted the knife. A blinding beam swept into the cooler.

"Captain Johnson?"

"You're late to the party, Pickens." He lowered the

knife as the lance corporal entered the cooler. "You didn't happen to see anyone suspicious lurking around outside, did you?"

"No, sir." His apprehension apparent, Pickens examined them both. "Are you the only one wounded, sir?"

"Did you encounter anyone else bleeding in the aisles?"

Pickens shook his head.

"Then I assume I'm the only one."

The power surged on, and it took a couple of seconds for his eyes to adjust. Olivia seized his hand and, tugging him out of the cooler, moved to get a closer look at his neck.

"Call a medic," she told Pickens.

"Yes, ma'am."

Olivia turned a complete circle, her gaze snagging on the paper towel dispenser. She used them to try to stem the bleeding. Her brow was knitted, her dark brows tucked together and her lower lip snagged between her teeth.

He reached up and gently tucked the sparkly hairpin back into place. Her eyes shifted to his, and the intensity of her worry for his well-being knocked the breath from his lungs.

"It's nothing more than a scratch, you know."

"If that were the case, there wouldn't be the need for a major cleanup in the dairy section."

"Look on the bright side," he quipped. "My guess is the manager will give us a discount for our trouble. More ice cream for us. He may even throw in some whipped cream and chocolate syrup for free."

An amused breath blew through her pursed lips. "This is a new side of you, Captain."

"You mean I'm not the humorless robot you pegged me for?"

The pressure she'd been applying to his neck went slack. Guilt slid through her eyes. Not the reaction he was going for. Before he could think of something to say, the manager bustled in. More MPs arrived, along with EMTs. They wanted to transport him to the naval hospital on Camp Lejeune, but he insisted on being treated at the scene. After his wound was cleaned and antibiotics applied, they used butterfly bandages instead of stitches.

He and Olivia gave a joint statement to the military police. When they were free to go, Pickens was on hand to follow them to base housing.

Olivia climbed into his truck but put her hand out to prevent him from closing the door. "I don't want to stay on base," she said, her gaze scanning the woods behind the commissary. "I know he's probably gone, but I won't sleep a wink in that house."

"We'll go to mine."

"You shouldn't be around me, Brady."

"Yes, I should. Now more than ever."

He closed the door and walked around to the driver's side. Before getting in, he tapped on Pickens's window. "We're going to my place. You can return to headquarters."

The lance corporal opened his mouth to argue, caught Brady's expression and nodded. "Yes, sir."

In his spot behind the wheel, Brady started the engine and pulled out of the lot.

"Take me to a hotel."

"No."

"It doesn't have to be in the city," she reasoned. "The one on Camp Lejeune probably has vacancies."

His hands tight on the wheel, Brady glanced over at her. "I am not leaving you, Olivia. Not now, not ever."

Her lips parted in surprise. He'd meant until this guy was no longer a threat, but he couldn't form the words. The ride to his neighborhood was completed in silence. They both kept watch for anyone tailing them. At his house, he quickly closed the garage door, reset the alarm and retrieved his gun from the safe. Returning from his bedroom, he found Olivia standing in the middle of the living room, her arms crisscrossed over her middle.

Her beauty had a bedraggled quality. The hairpin had come loose again. Her smoky eyeliner was smudged, and there was dried blood on her hands and a streak of it on her cheek. At his footfall, she turned and tried valiantly to offer him a smile. Her courage, her perseverance in the face of adversity, astounded him. Here she was, smack in the middle of a nightmare, and she was trying to make *him* feel better. To convince him with a smile that she was okay so he wouldn't worry.

Brady set the gun on the dining table and crossed the room to her.

"This hairpin does not want to stay in," he murmured, carefully slipping the strands free of the sparkly adornment. He watched the silken waves tumble past her ear. "Here you are."

He placed the pin into her palm. Head bowed, she curled her fingers around it. Unable to resist, he threaded his fingers through the waves and smoothed the mass behind her shoulder.

Brady shrugged out of his tuxedo jacket and settled it over her. He didn't let go of the lapels, though. The fabric securely in his grip, he slowly tugged her closer. He expected her to resist. To question what he was doing. Her eyes were locked onto his, and they were brimming with longing and wonder.

His heart hummed and soared in expectation.

How could this be? *Olivia.*

He didn't realize he'd said her name aloud until she responded.

"Yes?" Her face was angled upward, her lips a beacon in the night.

Brady touched his fingertips to the soft flesh. He skimmed her chin, her jaw, her uninjured cheek.

Her lids fluttered closed, and she leaned into him. "Brady."

His name was a reverent, awe-filled whisper. His chest swelled with gratitude. She liked him. She *cared* for him, something he hadn't thought possible.

Cupping her nape, he lowered his mouth to hers.

Silent accusation ripped through him. *You can't do this. Not with the secrets between you.*

Her lips clung to his like a quivering butterfly's wing, her entire being still, anticipating his next move.

Crushing his selfish instincts took almost more strength than he possessed. Olivia was a precious gift... someone he could depend on, someone he could trust. He didn't have to hide any part of himself from her. That's why he couldn't hurt her like this. Couldn't deceive her.

He broke the connection and released the lapels. She swayed, her eyes popping open, confusion glazing the brown depths.

"Brady?"

"I am so sorry."

"Sorry? Why?"

He trudged to the kitchen island and braced himself against the counter to stay upright. "Forgive me. I'm not certain how to explain."

She didn't speak for long, excruciating moments. "It's all right. I get it." Her half-hearted laugh had a mocking edge. "You're exhausted. Mentally and physically taxed. You wouldn't have kissed me if these had been normal circumstances. Not that we can label that a kiss. The start of one, maybe..."

Anguish crept into her voice, and he shifted around to face her.

Her fingers worked in her skirt, pleating and crush-

ing the gossamer material. "I mean, you didn't approve
of me before I became a target. This danger we've been
in, the trials we've faced together, skewed your opinion.
As soon as it's over, you'll want to go your own way. Re-
vert to how things used to be."

"No, Liv." He took a single step toward her, a terrible
ache building inside him.

"No." She lifted her arms to keep him at bay. "It's
okay. I don't want this. I was reckless before, with Derek.
I promised myself I wouldn't repeat the same mistakes."
Pushing her hair off her forehead, she said, "For years, I
immersed myself in my studies. While my classmates had
active social lives, I kept my nose buried in books. My
parents sacrificed to pay for my education, and I was determined to make them proud. I didn't go on a single date
in all that time. After graduation, I switched my focus to
building a career. But then Derek bumped into me, and
literally knocked my world off-kilter."

Brady knew the story by heart. She'd been shopping
in downtown Wilmington, located about an hour south of
Jacksonville, when Derek had accidentally collided with
her. He'd caused her to drop her bags. A birthday gift for
her mother had been damaged, and he'd insisted on pur-
chasing a replacement. Afterward, he'd convinced her to
get coffee with him. They'd been inseparable after that.

"He embarked on a quest to charm and dazzle me, and
he succeeded. I fell hard and fast. How could I not? Here
was this handsome, accomplished, brave marine, and for
whatever reason, he thought I was special."

"You *are* special."

"That's not the point. The thing is, Brady, I didn't enter
our marriage with a clear idea of who he was."

His heartbeat slowed. "What are you saying?"

"Not long after the wedding, I began to sense he was
holding something back. He avoided serious topics,

dodged most questions. I can't prove it, obviously, but I think he had secrets."

Brady closed his eyes and prayed for wisdom. When he'd promised his best friend that Olivia wouldn't learn of his past from him, he hadn't foreseen this scenario—a future without Derek, and Olivia with a price on her head.

He pushed off the island, his thoughts a tangled jumble. *Price on her head?*

"Maybe he knew there was something wrong with him," she mused. "Maybe that's why he was committed to leaching as much fun from each day as possible."

Brady began to pace. "I don't know why I didn't think of this before."

"Think of what?"

"These attempts on your life. I've made them out to be personal. A coworker with a grudge. Dr. Ledford and his unrequited crush. What if it's not personal at all?"

Olivia watched him with wary eyes. "You have a new theory?"

He stopped short, dreading what he had to do. He wished it hadn't come to this. Derek should've been the one to tell her, not him. But she might possess some seemingly inconsequential piece of information that could help them avoid future attacks.

Brady took her hands in his. "Olivia, there's something I have to tell you, and you're not going to like it."

She tensed. "You have an odd expression on your face, like you're about to deliver devastating news."

"Life-altering news," he said. "It's not mine to share, exactly, but the time has come."

"You're scaring me, Brady. Just spit it out."

He sucked in a ragged breath. "Your husband was not who he claimed to be. Derek Waters didn't exist. His actual name was Matteo Giordano, and he was the heir to a mafia empire."

FIFTEEN

Olivia jerked her hands free. "What are you saying?"

"In order to escape a life of crime, he had to fake his own death and create a new persona."

Brady's somber countenance, coupled with the regret in his stormy eyes, sliced her protests to ribbons. He wouldn't joke about this.

But Derek would. "Oh, Brady, don't you see? You've been duped. This is one of Derek's pranks. Clearly, he took it too far. He should've told you right away."

Her words didn't have the desired effect. "No, Liv. He had proof. I'll show it to you."

She followed him to the spare bedroom he'd converted to an office. She waited just inside the door, convinced it was an elaborate hoax. Derek had often played practical jokes on his buddies. This one wasn't well thought-out. In fact, it was cruel, and that was something her late husband hadn't been.

Brady removed a manila file from his filing cabinet. His jaw was tight, his countenance grave. He hadn't changed from his tuxedo, and dark russet stains marred his white dress shirt. Above his collar, bandages didn't completely hide his torn, bruised skin. She wasn't immune to him, despite the rawness of his rejection. Even now, she would give anything to be in his arms, to be welcomed and loved—

"Olivia?"

His voice jarred her from her musings. That she could be distracted by him in this moment told her how deep she'd gotten.

She took the file and flipped it open.

"These are newspaper articles relating to his death," he said. "The one he staged."

Olivia lowered herself into the desk chair and spread out the clippings, singling out one with a photo of a much younger Derek. She splayed her fingers over the likeness, shock and denial spiraling through her. "This can't be."

"I didn't believe it, either, at first," he said quietly. "When he went missing, his family offered reward money for information leading to his whereabouts. They located his car later, submerged in a local waterway. It bothered him that there was no body. He said his father wouldn't consider the case closed without concrete evidence. That's why social media made Derek nervous."

The words blurred on the page. "How did he pull it off?"

"He paid a trusted mafia contact to orchestrate the accident and provide him with the trappings of a new identity."

Her mind reeled. "He would've had to have a different social security number in order to enlist, right? A birth certificate and driver's license." Her husband had committed bribery and fraud. What other crimes didn't she know about?

"There are plenty of career criminals willing to provide illegal services for a price."

Olivia closed the file. "How can you be so calm?"

Apology turned his eyes an opaque gray. "Because I've lived with this revelation for more than a year."

She digested his words. "More than a year, huh?"

"Olivia—"

"When?"

He grimaced. "About a month before he died."

She closed her eyes. "I don't know how to feel, other than numb."

He touched her sleeve. She shrank away, shoving the chair back and jerking to her feet. She ripped off his jacket and tossed it his direction.

"I promised him, Liv."

"You helped him perpetuate a lie. To think, I married an imposter—" She clapped her hand over her mouth.

"I'm sorry," he intoned. "If I could go back and change things—"

Olivia whirled and sought the solitude of the guest bedroom. Engaging the lock, she carried the file to the bed and began ripping the pages into shreds.

Brady knocked on the door. "Olivia, don't shut me out. Please, let's talk about this."

Feeling hollow inside, she stretched out on the mattress atop the misshapen shreds and waited for tears that didn't come.

The doorbell woke him the next morning. Disoriented, Brady glanced at his watch and groaned. He'd overslept.

Hurrying through the house, he looked out the window and saw the car of his friend Julian's fiancée, Audrey, in the driveway. Right on time. Disabling the alarm, he swung the door open and bid her to follow him.

"Hey, Audrey. Thanks for agreeing to stay with Olivia."

"I'm happy to help," she said, sliding a pink box on the kitchen island. "Julian will bring lunch during his break." Still wearing her surgical scrubs from her overnight shift, she watched him pop a coffee pod into the machine and shove a mug under the drip spout. "You slept in your tux?"

"I dozed off on the couch and slept right through my alarm."

His gaze drifted to the hallway, his chest tight with helplessness. Had Olivia managed to get any rest? She hadn't agreed to speak with him. Not that he blamed her. He'd made a mess of things.

"Julian told me what happened in the commissary. You should've gone to the hospital for treatment." Her blue eyes were full of sympathy. Having been through her own nightmare, she could relate. "Be sure to keep it clean. They gave you antibiotic cream?"

"Yes."

"How's your hand? How many stitches did you get?"

Brady splashed milk into his coffee. "No time for the nurse routine," he said. "I'm running late."

Opening the box, she selected a glazed doughnut and held it aloft. "Julian had more of his sister's doughnuts shipped from Hawaii. You can't say no."

"I'll take it to go." He hesitated, uncertain how much to reveal. "Olivia's been under a lot of stress. Last night was rough."

She replaced the doughnut and cocked her head to one side, her long ponytail sliding over her shoulder. "Is there something you aren't telling me?"

Brady shouldn't be surprised at her insight. He'd spent a lot of time with her and Julian in recent months. "Yes."

She considered that. "I'll be here for whatever she needs."

Brady wished he could stick around, but considering Olivia's reaction last night, maybe space was a good thing. "I appreciate it, Audrey."

At her odd look, he said, "What?"

"You didn't say that you owed me."

"Huh?"

"You tend to view things in terms of repayment. Someone helps you out, you plan a way to return the favor. This time, you expressed gratitude. That's progress."

"I suppose."

"Being around Olivia has been good for you."

"But can she say the opposite is true?"

He walked to the end of the hallway and stopped before her door. He debated knocking. If she was asleep, he didn't want to wake her. It didn't feel right leaving without speaking to her, however.

Brady lifted his hand, only to realize the door wasn't completely closed. Odd. She'd made sure it was locked last night. He nudged it open a couple of inches.

"Olivia? Are you awake?" In the ensuing silence, he said, "I'm coming in."

Slowly, he pushed the door all the way open. The bed was empty, the covers smoothed and pillows plumped.

His heart slammed against his chest. Adrenaline spiked. He tore through the room, searching for clues. Her things were gone. The window was locked, the alarm system tabs in place. Surely if someone had breached the house and taken her, he would've heard something.

Then his gaze snagged on a piece of paper on the carpet. A sense of foreboding closing up his airway, he read the brief message.

Olivia was fine, if the note was to be believed. She simply couldn't remain in his home. She'd taken a cab to the air station sometime during the night and didn't wish to be contacted.

Brady crumpled the paper in his fist. She knew the alarm code. He must've been under a heavy blanket of fatigue not to hear her.

Fishing out his phone, he typed out a text asking if she'd gotten home safely.

"Brady, there's someone pulling in…" Audrey's voice trailed off. "Where is she?"

Scowling at his phone, he waved the note. "Apparently,

she took a taxi to her place, but she's not answering. I have to go and check on her."

"She could be asleep," she pointed out as he brushed past her.

"Or she could be in the hands of a killer."

Her enemy hadn't been afraid to try to run them off the road before. He wouldn't balk at doing the same to a taxi.

Brady pulled on his shoes, retrieved his weapon and opened the garage. He was leaving a message with the next in the chain of command, Major Falk, letting him know he'd be late, when he noticed the visitor.

"Lieutenant Colonel." He left the garage just as a brisk breeze whipped around him. "What brings you here?"

Lieutenant Colonel Russell's astute gaze swept over Brady, taking in every single detail. Stubble on his jaw, rumpled, bloodstained shirt and wrinkled pants.

"You've been grounded, Johnson."

"Sir?"

"This isn't a punishment. Your safety, and that of the marines under my command, is my chief priority."

"You heard about the commissary incident."

"The squadron's abuzz." Nodding to Brady's bandages, he said, "You have vacation time. Take it. Figure out what's best for you and Olivia while you're waiting for law enforcement to nab this guy."

"Sir, I—"

"You're a reasonable man," he interrupted, clapping him on the shoulder. "You'll agree this is best for everyone."

Brady pinched the bridge of his nose. He felt a headache coming on. *Grounded.* He finally understood why Olivia fought to stay at the aquarium. This felt like giving up, like letting the enemy win.

"Putting anyone in danger is the last thing I want," he said at last.

"Give it time. I have faith it will all work out in the end."

"Yes, sir."

The older man returned to his vehicle. Halfway into his seat, he paused. "Keep me updated."

"Will do."

Brady went inside and informed Audrey that she was free to go. She attempted to cheer him up by forcing a doughnut into his hands. He took it and his coffee on the road. Right now he couldn't dwell on his work status. Olivia's well-being was all that mattered.

The marine at the main gate gave him a stern look when he caught sight of his unshaven state, but he waved him through. The ride through the base seemed to take a lifetime, thanks to the morning rush hour and the restricted speed limit. Finally, he reached the housing area.

At the sight of the military police cruiser in her driveway, the vise around his chest eased somewhat. Corporal Baker exited the car and waited for him to park.

"Good morning, Captain. I'm supposed to inform you that she isn't taking visitors."

Brady shut his door and engaged the lock. "I appreciate that you're doing your job, but I'm not leaving until I see her."

Baker's chin was set at a defiant angle, but beneath her cover's brim, her eyes were searching. He sensed she wasn't simply following orders. She liked Olivia and empathized with her situation.

"Were you here when she arrived?" he said.

"No, but I've spoken to her this morning. She looks about like you do."

"Oh? How's that?"

"Like you both need a long vacation."

He didn't bother telling her his had started half an hour ago. She had spunk, this one. A helpful trait in a male-dominated career.

"I need to see for myself that she's okay."

The corporal's eyes narrowed before a sigh gusted out of her. "Don't make her day any worse."

He kept his mouth shut because he couldn't make that promise. In the time it took for Olivia to answer the door-bell, his palms grew clammy, and he wished he'd taken the time to freshen up.

Then the knob was turning, the door swinging inward, and Olivia stood before him. Close enough to touch. To pull into his arms.

"Brady." Her voice was flat, her expression guarded. "Didn't you get my note?"

He nodded. "You didn't respond to my text, so I hopped in the truck and came straight over."

"My phone's on the charger. I didn't hear the notification." Still blocking the entrance, she gestured to the airfield's general direction. "Aren't you supposed to be at work?"

"The lieutenant colonel paid me a personal visit this morning. I've been ordered to take my vacation days."

Her posture lost some of its starch. "I'm sorry, Brady. I really am. You should tell him that you're no longer my personal bodyguard. Maybe he'll reconsider."

"That would be a lie."

Her lips pursed, and her fingernails dug into the door frame. "I don't have the energy to debate the issue."

She started to close the door. Brady's arm shot out. "Olivia, please. Give me a chance to explain."

Frowning, she turned and retreated. He let himself in, closed the door and stared at the mess. Where before there'd been relative order, the cardboard boxes were now in disarray and belongings strewn on the couch, coffee table and dining table.

She rifled through stacks of papers. "I've spent the last several hours poring over Derek's stuff, and I haven't found a single thing to link him to this Giordano mafia family."

He sank his hands into his pockets. "He'd had years of practice hiding his past. I don't know that he kept anything that could link him to them."

"Did he tell you why he took such drastic measures?"

"His older brother was destined to take over for his father someday, leaving Derek free to pursue a normal life. He'd planned to leave New Jersey and attend university on the West Coast. But then Antonio was gunned down by a rival family, and Derek was expected to take his place."

"I'm guessing he balked." Her eyes desolate, she shook her head. "He was capable of many things, but violence—life as a mafia man—wasn't one of them."

"The fact that he chose the Marines speaks volumes. He wanted to affect good in the world."

"I wonder if he would've ever told me." She scrubbed her hands down her face.

He used the coffee table for a seat. "I believe he would have, eventually." At her disbelieving stare, he shrugged. "He and I argued about it. As his wife, you deserved to know."

"And yet you didn't tell me, even after he was gone."

"At first, you were in shock. We both were. And then you were attempting to rebuild your life. I couldn't shatter you all over again while dishonoring my best friend's memory."

Her lips formed a tight line of distress. Running her

fingers along the cast's uneven surface, she said, "How could I have not sensed something was off?"

"He and I were friends for years. Not once did I suspect he wasn't Derek Waters from Richmond, Virginia."

Her gaze stabbed him. "You didn't live with the man."

"The fact that you were his wife makes you a target. He could've shared damaging family secrets with you."

"That's ridiculous." Bolting to her feet, she began to haphazardly stuff items into boxes. "I didn't know his real name, let alone mafia secrets."

Brady stood. "They don't know that. According to Derek, these aren't the kind of people to overlook threats to their livelihoods, no matter how trivial."

"The Giordanos think he's dead."

"Derek slipped up. Using a computer at the city library, he searched social media for information about his little sister and mother. His curiosity got the better of him. That was months before he met you. I'd forgotten about it until the subject of Derek's real identity came up last night."

"It's hardly likely that one internet search would lead them to him."

"Maybe. But it might have gotten someone's attention. But according to Derek, his father is a proud, ruthless man. He won't give up until he has proof of Derek's death."

"If it is them behind the attacks, they know he's gone. For real, this time."

"They don't know what he told you about their business."

"I'm not convinced."

"Olivia, whether or not I'm right, the danger is far from over. We've got to stick together."

She didn't answer for a long time. "For the time being, we do it your way."

The breath whooshed out of him.

"But as far as I'm concerned, this arrangement is strictly for our mutual survival. Don't try and be my friend or—" her throat convulsed "—or anything else."

Brady masked his anguish. He had to put Olivia's wants and needs before his own. She required time to sort through her hurt, disillusionment and anger. Distance, too, but he couldn't give her that. One thing was certain— he wouldn't ever stop trying to regain her trust.

SIXTEEN

Four days after Brady's confession, Olivia's perspective began to right itself. She figured out why it was easy to direct her anger at him. He was a convenient target and, thanks to his childhood wounds, willing to bear the blame. The one who was truly at fault, the one who'd wooed, charmed and ultimately married her under false pretenses wasn't around. She hoped to eventually come to terms with Derek's drastic choices. For the time being, she had to deal with the fallout while guarding her heart from the wide range of emotions Brady inspired in her.

"I thought it wasn't supposed to rain until tonight." Crouched in the far side of the stream, Erin glared up at the sky. Her hip waders were streaked with mud, and her slick jacket showed evidence of her claim.

Rain began to pelt the forest, disturbing the murky water's surface. Grayish-white clouds stretched above them. Olivia finished measuring the last green sunfish and returned it to the bucket. She recorded the data on her chart.

"At least it held off until we finished our last section." Field days were a perk of the job, a chance to get outdoors and interact with nature. She'd signed on for this excursion to survey local fish populations before Ruth had banned her from the aquarium.

Erin sloshed out of the water and pointed to the line of buckets. "You're ready for me to release these, right?"

Nodding, she tucked her ruler into her plastic container.

"I've identified the various species and measured the fish. I didn't find any invasive ones."

She made a grunt of satisfaction. In between buckets, she gestured upstream.

"Your bodyguard's probably ready to leave."

Olivia spared a glance at Brady. He'd passed the hours pacing along the stream, scanning the woods for potential threats and occasionally consulting his phone.

"You could've accepted his offer to assist," she said. "He must be bored out of his mind."

"He's planning a project in his backyard and brought construction magazines with him. He could've used the time to research ideas."

"You and he were chummy at the gala. You've barely spoken to each other today." Her gaze roamed Olivia's face. "Want to talk about it?"

The memory of dancing with Brady was a bittersweet one. Then, she hadn't known about the secret he'd been keeping from her.

"Not really. I'll contact the other team." Olivia moved closer to a towering pine tree in an effort to protect her screen from raindrops. She sent a text and received an almost immediate response. "They're already in their truck and ready to head out. They're asking if we want them to wait."

"No need." Erin swiped moisture from her face. "It'll take us a solid fifteen minutes to gather our seine nets and another ten to walk back."

Olivia sent the response and slid her cell into her jacket pocket. Working quickly, she removed the vertical nets they'd placed in intervals along the stream. Erin stacked the buckets and retrieved a stray dip net. They both removed their cumbersome waders.

"I'll let Brady know we're ready." He'd helped them

transport their gear to the site earlier and had promised to lend a hand when they'd finished.

Before she could take a step, the report of a rifle cracked through the trees. Erin cried out. Her eyes bulged, and she doubled over. Olivia slung her arm around her and hustled her behind the pine.

"Where are you hurt?"

Erin gulped in air and sat down hard, her back to the trunk. "My side."

Brady skidded in beside them, his weapon drawn. His intense gaze evaluated Olivia first before cutting to Erin. "How bad is it?"

"I don't know." Olivia hunched down and shifted Erin's jacket aside. Blood seeped through her shirt.

"Check to see if there's an exit wound," he instructed, his back to them.

Lifting Erin's jacket, she checked. "No."

Erin's face crumpled. "That's bad, isn't it? The bullet's lodged inside."

Tugging off her jacket, Olivia folded it in half and pushed it against the wound. Erin whimpered. "Sorry. We have to slow the bleeding."

Brady punched in a number and spoke to emergency dispatch. When he'd finished, he glanced over his shoulder. "A downtown business is on fire. Emergency personnel have their hands full battling that and rerouting traffic. Someone will come, but it won't be soon. We'll have to get her to the truck and take her ourselves."

"I can take the gun and provide cover if you want to carry her."

His jaw was tight enough to bounce nails off of. "Bad idea."

"Because I haven't handled a weapon before?"

He shook his head. "We're dealing with a professional here."

As if to reinforce his argument, the bark above their heads exploded. Brady returned fire, then lunged to shield them. The ensuing quiet was broken by the incessant ping of raindrops.

"He's not wasting his ammo," he bit out. "He's cool-headed and methodical, a deadly combination. We have to move."

"I...I can walk on my own," Erin said.

Olivia put her arm around Erin's waist. "Lean on me."

Her complexion turned grayish when they got to their feet. She gritted her teeth. "Which way?"

Brady motioned across the stream. "He'll expect us to take the obvious route to the vehicle. We'll have to take a circuitous one."

Olivia's hold on Erin tightened. "Ready?"

With Brady providing cover, they navigated the shallow water and slippery rocks and entered the woods. The pines and other evergreens created a natural umbrella, causing the rain to fall in a haphazard pattern. Anxiety wound her insides into taut knots, and the need to run full steam dogged her. Olivia kept looking over her shoulder. When would the next bullet zoom through the trees and find its mark?

She and Erin went first, picking their way through the slippery carpet of leaves and soft earth. Much of the underbrush hadn't yet succumbed to autumn's cold, and the vegetation was chest high in places. Brady walked several steps behind them, keeping himself between them and the shooter's last location. Erin's initial determination began to flag and her strength wane. There was no way to know if hiking through the forest would cause more damage to her internal organs.

Olivia stopped. "How much farther until we can change direction?"

Dragging his gaze from the terrain they'd covered, he turned around and studied Erin with a grim turn to his mouth.

"We haven't traveled far. Maybe half a mile."

"It's okay," Erin said slowly, squeezing her eyes tight. "I can keep going."

A hollow crack was chased by a whistling bullet. It whizzed past Olivia, inches from her head, and dug into the ground.

"Run!" Brady barked as the shooter continued to open fire.

They dashed through the trees as fast as Erin's injury allowed. Brady got off several shots. They stumbled upon a rusted-out canoe and, farther on, a dilapidated shack and empty dog houses.

Erin clutched her middle. "I have to rest for a minute."

"Get behind that shack." Brady ducked behind the canoe.

Erin leaned more heavily on Olivia. Once they'd reached the far side of the ramshackle building, her knees gave out and she slid to the ground.

"I'm sorry." Tears leaked from her eyes.

Olivia clutched her hand, guilt a paralyzing weight. While she'd given Erin the option of joining the other team, this was her fault.

"You've nothing to apologize for."

Her eyes closed. "I'm slowing you down."

"We are going to reach the truck, and we are going to get you to the hospital." There was no other acceptable outcome.

The exchange of gunfire pierced the stillness. Olivia

flinched. Brady was in a precarious position, with nothing but a rotted-out boat to protect him.

Please, Father, lead us to safety.

When he sprinted around the corner unharmed, relief eclipsed despair.

"How is she?"

Olivia gently nudged Erin's hand out of the way. The bleeding had increased at a faster rate than she'd hoped.

"We need a different plan."

His expression turned grimmer. "Let me carry her."

"While you also fend off the shooter?" Erin gasped. "No thanks."

"We'll split up," he said. "I'll draw him away while you two return to the truck. It's almost dark. The gathering shadows will hinder his sight."

"I don't like it," Olivia said.

"It's our best option."

"What if you get shot, too? On your own, you could bleed out or get disoriented and lose your way."

Raindrops slid down his cheek and dripped off his chin. His wet hair was plastered to his head. His blue-gray eyes, when they regarded her, communicated sadness and regret. It was the same expression he'd worn for days, only now it gutted her. Because if they split up, there was no guarantee she'd see him again.

"I'll have my phone." He inclined his head toward Erin. "We don't have time to waste."

Olivia didn't speak as he helped Erin to her feet. She listened as he explained the exact route they should take.

"When you reach the truck, don't wait for me." He shucked off his jacket and insisted she put it on. "Get her to the hospital and stay with security."

She seized his wrist. "Promise me you'll be careful."

His gaze clinging to hers, he nodded. "I promise."

* * *

Brady hated this plan, but Erin's slow progress wouldn't allow them to reach safety otherwise. He instructed them to wait five minutes before heading out. Olivia's guarded veil slipped for the first time in days, and what he saw in her eyes gave him hope. Maybe she didn't despise him, after all. Maybe the damage he'd inflicted could be repaired. Maybe she'd look at him like she had at the gala and later, in his living room—like he was worthy of her admiration.

Praying for the Lord's protection for them all, he started through the trees without trying to mask his whereabouts. The shooter's responding shot told him he'd taken the bait. Good. He had to lure him away and give the women enough time to reach the company truck.

He hiked at an uneven speed to let the shooter think Erin was there, too. The distant crunch of leaves and occasional snap of a branch reassured him that he was in pursuit. Brady wound between the trees until he reached the water, farther downstream from where they'd been earlier. Dusk was complete, the sky overhead a bruised grayish purple. At least the cold rain had stopped. Hunkering at the tree's base, he tossed a stick into the stream and waited for the shooter's response.

He waited in vain. Brady shoved upright and examined the woods that spread out around him in a painter's study of dreary browns. The silence was excruciating.

Was he out there, obscured by the underbrush, his sights trained on Brady? Or had he figured out the ruse?

His gut clenched. With no other option, he sprinted into the clearing and splashed through the stream, his body braced for an onslaught. He reached the other side convinced he was alone.

The enemy had gone after Olivia.

* * *

"There's the truck," she gasped, her upper back protesting Erin's weight. The woods had thinned suddenly and opened into a clearing that revealed the gravel access road.

Her friend grunted a response. She was hovering on the edge of consciousness.

Wedging her shoulder more firmly against Erin, Olivia readjusted her hold on her waist. "All we have to do is cross the stream, okay? Then we're out of here."

Getting Erin medical attention was paramount, but that didn't mean she was okay with abandoning Brady.

"Erin?"

"Mmm."

Her eyes were closed, her mouth slack. *Please, Lord Jesus, let her stay conscious long enough to reach the truck.*

"Stay with me, Erin."

Olivia urged her forward. Their progress was erratic and painstaking. Once, in the midst of the stream, Erin almost slipped from her grasp. Somehow, she managed to keep her upright. She half dragged her the rest of the way.

"Thank you, Jesus." Opening the passenger door, Olivia got her into the seat. She was about to secure the seat belt when a masked figure rounded the truck's front.

Olivia's mouth opened in a silent scream. Slamming the door, she backed away, her hands up.

The long-range rifle was slung around his back. He raised his arm and pointed a handgun at her head.

She was moments away from death. Brady would forever believe she didn't care enough to extend grace and forgiveness. He'd never know how her feelings for him had changed or how much that frightened her.

The gun fired, and her scream blasted through the forest.

SEVENTEEN

The anticipated pain didn't register.

"Olivia! Run!"

The gunman seized her arm before she could make out that Brady had fired a shot. He missed, however. Too much ground separated them. The gunman jerked her behind the truck and propelled her away from the access road.

She attempted to impede his progress, digging in her feet and grasping at branches. His grip was like an iron manacle. She glimpsed a beat-up sedan deliberately hidden by tree limbs, and her stomach sank. He shoved her against the car, her forehead cracking against the window. Black dots danced in her vision. Fisting his hand in her hair, he dragged her around to the back and popped the trunk.

Panic slithered through her. What did the news articles always say? Never get into the car with an abductor.

"Brady! Over here!"

The gunman growled and yanked her hair so hard it brought tears to her eyes. She wasn't about to give up. She slammed her heel into his shin. Elbowed him in the ribs. Swung her cast up and around, but he ducked out of reach.

His fingers digging into her arms, he pushed her upper body into the trunk space. The stench of seawater assaulted her nose the moment her face met the rough carpet-like interior. She gagged.

He caught her ankles and lifted her legs.

Gunfire crackled through the woods. He howled and dropped her, stumbling and clutching his shoulder. A bullet must've struck him.

"Olivia!"

She scrambled out of the trunk cavity in time to see the gunman spin and prepare to shoot. Brady was already there, however. He tackled the gunman to the ground. The gun skittered out of reach. They rolled. Exchanged blows.

Olivia finally thought to search for the gun. She tore through the leaves, desperation making her sloppy.

Behind her, the commotion ceased and an engine growled to life. The car lurched forward. Spinning in a wide arc, it gained speed and rumbled over the terrain.

Brady fired at the fleeing vehicle. The rear windshield shattered. The car didn't slow, however.

Olivia jogged over to Brady. "Are you hurt?"

His lower lip was busted, and there was a tiny cut above his eyebrow. His chest heaved. "No. You?"

She shook her head and wished she hadn't. A massive headache was forming behind her eyes. "Erin's in the truck."

"I saw her. She was unconscious."

They broke into a run, retracing their route. The wail of sirens could be heard in the distance. Olivia slid onto the bench seat.

"Erin? Can you hear me?"

Her head was propped against the window, her eyes closed and pulse erratic.

Brady got in, closed the door and engaged the locks.

"She's lost too much blood," Olivia murmured, renewed fear gripping her.

"The hospital's not far."

He guided the truck over the bumpy gravel. At the

main road, he braked hard. Olivia used the dashboard to brace herself. Sirens wailed louder. An ambulance raced their direction.

When it began to slow, she said, "I think that's for us."

Brady parked and waved them down. Together, they relayed what happened as the EMTs got Erin onto a gurney. A pair of patrol cars arrived on the scene, and drawing them away from the ambulance, the officers took their statements. A crime scene unit was called in.

Olivia watched the ambulance leave. "I'd hoped to get some idea of her condition before they left."

"Are we free to go, Officer?" Brady asked.

"You should have an escort. Give me a few minutes, and I'll follow you."

He went to speak to his fellow officer, and Brady guided her to the truck. He opened the passenger door. At the sight of the blood, tears threatened.

"I should never have come."

He urged her around, tugged her against his chest and twined his arms around her. "This isn't the time to second-guess ourselves. Erin's young, fit and healthy. We have to think positively."

She pressed her cheek to his pounding heart. "When he pointed that gun at me—" A shudder wracked her body. "I have to tell you something."

Tensing, he tried to pull away and look at her, but she wouldn't budge. "Liv?"

"Blaming you for Derek's decisions was wrong. I don't hold you accountable. I want you to know that."

His hands slid up her back, pressing her closer. "You and I weren't exactly close when I made that ill-conceived promise. I regret hurting you."

Olivia angled her head up and met his emotion-charged perusal. "Friends again?"

"You have my friendship, always."

Friendship should've been enough. Mere weeks ago, it would've been. But she couldn't focus on that. Her past mistakes proved she couldn't trust her judgment when it came to matters of the heart.

When they were told that Erin wouldn't be out of surgery for a while, Olivia suggested they go to the hospital chapel. They prayed aloud together, a first for Brady. He'd taken part in his church's Bible study groups, of course, but praying with another person—Olivia in particular— was a more intimate experience. He was deeply grateful she'd had a change of heart. He'd borne the disappointment of others, but Olivia's had been gut-wrenching.

They left the chapel and were greeted by Corporal Baker. He almost didn't recognize her in her civilian clothes.

"Captain. Olivia. I got your text as I was leaving the base." Her expression somber, she lifted a white paper sack. "I brought sandwiches from my favorite deli."

"That was thoughtful of you," Olivia told her.

"Please, call me Brady."

"Yes, sir. I mean, I'll try."

"We were heading upstairs to the waiting area," Olivia said. "Come with us."

On the elevator, she inquired after Erin's condition.

"She's in surgery. We haven't received any updates."

When they'd reached the correct floor, Brady purchased sodas from the vending machine and joined the women in the deserted waiting area. Olivia received a phone call from her mom midway through their meal. He was able to see her through the window to the hallway.

"Does she know how you feel?"

He set down his sub sandwich and deliberately wiped his fingers with a napkin. "I'm not sure I know what you mean."

"I think you do." Cat's gaze was frank and appraising. "But it's none of my business. Forget I said anything. I've never been good at keeping my thoughts to myself."

Brady sat back in his chair and took a long draw on his soda. His feelings for Olivia weren't up for discussion. "She said you're new to the area. I've got a couple of buddies stationed in Okinawa." He rattled them off.

Her gaze skittering away, she tapped the table with her folded napkin. "I don't recognize the names."

"They love island life and aren't eager to return stateside. Were you sorry to leave?"

"Not at all. In fact, I hope to avoid that place in the future." Scooting her chair back, she stood and dropped the now crushed napkin into the empty sack. "I'm in the mood for something sweet. The cafeteria or gift shop should have something appetizing. Can I get you a candy bar? Ice cream?"

"No, thanks."

Olivia returned moments later. "Cat was in a hurry. Is she leaving?"

"She's on the hunt for a sugar fix. Did she talk to you about her last duty station?"

She resumed her seat across from him. "No, but I get the feeling something tainted her experience there."

"I think you may be right."

"Cat's been an unexpected source of support."

"Seems as though she could use a friend like you." He finished off his sandwich and placed the wrapper in the sack. "How's your mom?"

"Worried out of her mind. We spoke for hours last night. I told her everything."

"Everything?"

Her eyes darkened. "I left out the part about me being

married to an imposter. That's not something you tell someone over the phone."

"Understandable. That must've been difficult for her."

"She insisted I come home. When I refused, she switched tactics and told me to go to Charleston. My aunt and uncle have a small vacation cottage there. I've got to admit, the idea has merit."

The thought of her leaving Jacksonville for any length of time filled him with dread. "You'd be more vulnerable in a new place."

"On the flip side, it could help the case. Shaw would have time to work through the leads instead of dealing with constant attacks." Her eyes were sad. "If I were the only one in danger, I wouldn't consider it. But you've been in the line of fire again and again. Erin's in there fighting for her life as we speak. I think this may be the best option."

From the sound of things, she'd made up her mind. "What about your new apartment? You've already paid a deposit and signed a year's lease."

"This would be temporary. I will have to return to work. Unless they fire me, of course."

"That's not going to happen. Your contributions are too valuable."

"With me out of town, you can get back to work, too."

"It would be reckless for me to fly. I'd be worrying about you every second."

"You're too good of a pilot, too good a marine, to let anything distract you from your mission." She moved to cover his hand but pulled her hand back. "Would you agree to fly me down there? If I decide to go?"

Bleakness overtook his soul. Olivia had become an integral part of his life, so much so that he couldn't imagine his world without her in it.

EIGHTEEN

Her request had clearly shaken him. Olivia didn't want to leave any of it, not her work at the aquarium, not her friends or her church. Most of all, she didn't want to leave Brady.

What other choice did she have, though? The danger was escalating. Erin was fighting for her life. It was only by God's grace that she and Brady weren't in the same position. Her enemy had come close to shooting them both point-blank. Her throat began to close.

Refusing to let the panic gain control, she looked him square in the eye. "Well?"

His fingers gripped the soda can so hard, dents appeared in the sides. "*If* you decide to go, I'll take you."

The waiting room door swung open, and a young man lumbered inside, his head and shoulders bent. Shoving his longish hair off his forehead, he took stock of the cushioned chairs and magazines fanned out on side tables. He belatedly noticed them and froze.

"What are you doing here?" he barked, his voice hoarse.

Olivia recognized him at once. Erin's boyfriend. "Carson?" She left her chair and walked over. "Did the hospital contact you?"

"Erin's mom called me. She's driving up from Wilmington." His amber eyes hot with accusation, his hands fists at his sides. "If I were you, I'd leave before she gets here."

Brady came to stand slightly in front of Olivia, his hands on his hips. "Who are you, exactly?"

"Carson Ackerman, Erin's boyfriend."

"I'm so sorry about what happened," Olivia began.

"She told me what's been going on," he interrupted. "When I found out where she was going today and that she'd be with you, I warned her. I told her to call the director and refuse to work with you. Erin defended you. She's loyal. Too loyal, clearly."

"I understand you're upset," Brady said. "But blaming Olivia won't solve anything. It won't make you feel better and certainly won't help Erin."

"I gave her the option of joining the other team," Olivia said. "In hindsight, I should've insisted."

Carson's gaze turned despairing. "Yes, you should have."

The door opened, and a group of strangers entered. They must've sensed the tension, because they gave them a wide berth and chose seats on the opposite side of the room.

"Can you please leave?" Carson charged. "I don't want you here, and neither will Erin's family."

Brady bristled. "That's hardly fair."

She put her hand on his arm. "It's all right."

"No, it isn't."

"I don't want to cause anyone further distress." Her heart heavy, she returned to the table, discarded her trash and retrieved her phone. Coming even with Carson, she said, "You all have my prayers. I truly am sorry Erin got caught in the middle."

Brady's hand rested against her back, warm and comforting. Cat stepped off the elevator as they were about to enter, and they relayed what happened. Like Brady, she was unhappy with Carson's behavior.

"You don't have to leave," she said.

"I'm not. I'm going to wait somewhere else until Erin's out of surgery and I've heard her prognosis."

They exited into the first-floor lobby and were debating where to wait when Detective Shaw hailed them.

"Can I have a word?"

She couldn't decipher his expression. If he'd learned something useful, surely he'd look more upbeat.

"Call or text anytime," Cat told her. "Before or after the big move."

Olivia hugged her. "We'll stay in touch."

Cat and Brady shook hands. He thanked her for her help. After she'd left, they chose a quiet corner of the cafeteria. Shaw slid into the booth seat opposite them.

"Did you find anything useful?" Olivia blurted. "Clues to his identity and address?"

"I wish I could say we had something definitive to go on. We found a handgun with the serial number scraped off. That could point to gang involvement."

Brady shifted toward her. "Didn't you say Maya's boyfriend could be part of a gang?"

"He has a gang-related tattoo I read about in the newspaper. I've barely said hello to the guy."

Shaw pulled out a notebook and flipped through the pages. "Maya Fentress? Your coworker?"

"That's right."

"She resents you," Brady said. "Her attitude is antagonistic, at best."

"Maya's a good person. I can't accept she'd put her boyfriend up to this."

Shaw was jotting notes. "Could be she vented her frustrations to him, and he took it upon himself to fix her problems. Give me his name, and I'll look into it."

Olivia wasn't convinced, but she told him the requested information. "I gave the officers a description of the shooter's vehicle. Any leads on that?"

"They've issued a BOLO on the make and model. Neither of you got a plate number?"

"Everything happened so fast." She snapped her fingers. "I forgot to mention that the trunk smelled like the sea."

His brows rose. "Can you be more specific?"

"It was a salty, briny smell."

Beneath the table, Brady's hand found hers. She flipped hers over so that their palms fit together.

"I'll tell the others to focus on the waterfront areas. Our perp could be employed by a local fishing enterprise or seafood market." Shaw wrote more notes. "CSU will be at the site for a while yet. They're making casts of footprints and measuring tire treads."

"What about the slug pulled out of Julian's car?" Brady said.

"Nothing concrete, I'm afraid. After this, I'll pay the aquarium veterinarian, Zach Ledford, a visit."

"If he has a gunshot wound, he's our man."

"We're checking with hospitals as far north as New Bern and as far south as Wilmington. If our guy has sought medical treatment, we'll find out about it. He'll be more likely to do that if he's a lone wolf. Gangs take care of their own."

"Thank you, Detective." Olivia drummed up a smile.

He closed his notebook, capped his pen and regarded them both with unconcealed admiration. "You two are handling this surprisingly well. I've had people crumble under far less intense circumstances."

"I can't speak for Olivia, of course. My faith is the key.

While God is my creator and savior, He's also a friend who knows me inside and out and knows exactly what I need, when I need it."

Olivia gave his hand a light squeeze. "It's the same for me. He's my anchor in the storm."

When Detective Shaw left, Olivia angled toward Brady. "I'm going to miss you, you know."

His eyes narrowed. "What do you mean?"

"I can't stay here."

His lips compressed into a tight line. A battle waged in his eyes. At first, she thought he might protest. "I don't agree it's the best plan, but I'll respect your wishes."

"It's the safest course for everyone."

"You mean it's the safest course for everyone except for you."

Brady stowed her suitcases in the truck bed and climbed behind the wheel. In the early dawn's light, his eyes searched hers. "You're still set on going?"

The thought of being apart from him tore at her. But staying would be selfish. Every minute he was with her was another minute he was in danger. "I'm not leaving for good. I'll need for you to come and get me once this blows over."

He pressed the garage door opener and put the gear into Reverse. "Just say the word, and I'll be there."

As they left Brady's home, Olivia's emotions threatened to spill over. She trusted him with her life and knew she could count on him in any circumstance. She realized that, secret or no, she hadn't had that with Derek. In fact, she wouldn't want anyone else by her side.

"Julian said for you to call him when we get to Charleston."

He and Audrey, along with several guys from the

squadron, had moved her belongings into a storage unit. As much as she would've liked to have everything squared away in her new apartment, it was too dangerous.

"He texted me."

"Are you looking forward to seeing Hawaii?" According to Audrey, it had taken some persuading for Brady to agree to be Julian's best man.

"I try not to get excited about future events. You never know if they'll actually happen."

That was due to his parents' irresponsible, self-centered behavior, she was sure. "There's something to be said for taking life one day at a time. I'm a planner, though, so it's hard for me not to think about the future."

Her current circumstances didn't allow for such luxuries. God's Word said no one was promised tomorrow. Never before had that truth become impressed on her.

Ten minutes into their drive, his exclamation of disgust snapped her out of her increasingly morose thoughts.

"We may have a tail."

Trepidation zipping along her nerves, she checked the side mirror. "Is it the same car from the woods?"

"Looks like the one that tried to run us off the road."

She pulled out her phone. "Should I call emergency dispatch?"

His jaw rock hard, he made multiple lane changes. "Do it."

Olivia called and explained the situation. The dispatcher asked her to remain on the line and describe their location.

"I'm going to try and lose him before he starts shooting at us." He braked hard. "Hold on."

She held fast to the door grip as he whipped the truck into a right turn. The tires skidded and the rear end rocked. In the rearview mirror, she saw the car zip along the main road.

"He didn't follow us."

Confusion warred with relief.

Brady eased off the gas. At the next intersection, the light turned red, and he slowed to a stop.

She was about to disconnect the phone call when she spotted the car approaching from the right.

"Brady, look!"

They were blocked in, with a car in front and back, waiting for the light to turn green. "But I can't do anything about it."

The black behemoth slowed as it came near. Tinted windows hindered their view of the driver.

"What if he has a gun?"

Brady's eyes locked with hers. "We bail and run."

NINETEEN

"On second thought—"

Brady edged into the oncoming lane and executed a U-turn, then gunned the engine. He raced through the streets and, spying the bypass, joined the rush-hour traffic heading south. Olivia kept watch through the rear window.

"I don't see him."

Emergency dispatch advised them to go to the police station. Brady agreed and, changing direction at the next opportunity, drove into the heart of Jacksonville. On the way, Olivia texted Detective Shaw. He emerged from the building the moment they turned into the parking lot.

Brady parked and rolled down his window.

"Having trouble getting out of town?" Shaw said.

"You could say that."

"I'll escort you to the airport. Meanwhile, I've put a BOLO out for his vehicle." He leaned closer and, bracing himself against the side mirror, met Olivia's gaze. "I was going to call you. The tan Oldsmobile he was driving in the woods was stolen weeks ago, outside a waterfront tattoo parlor. I've got an officer over there checking the security footage. Maybe we'll get a break."

She longed for normalcy, to feel safe again.

Shaw got into his vehicle and followed them to the airport. Brady stuck to less-traveled secondary roads this time.

"I don't like the idea of you being alone down there."

His voice sliced through the thick silence. "I'm already using vacation days. Why don't I stick around?"

Olivia considered the possibilities. In the end, she chose to be rational. Because she hadn't been with Derek. She'd been swept away by the romance and flattery of his focused pursuit.

This is nothing like that, an inner voice insisted. This situation was very different. Brady was a different man. *A better man*. The words formed in her mind unbidden.

"I, uh, think you should return to work." Her voice sounded gravelly. "You don't want to waste your vacation days with me."

"They wouldn't be wasted," he protested.

She fisted her hands in her lap and stared out the side window. "Let's just leave things as we originally planned."

"Okay."

There was no denying his disappointment. At the general aviation facility, which was connected to the regional airport, Detective Shaw and Olivia remained in the building's waiting area while Brady checked in with the staff and conducted a thorough preflight check.

"I heard your friend got released yesterday."

Olivia watched another passenger jet roll down the distant runway. "Erin texted to let me know."

She'd apologized for her boyfriend's hostility. Apparently, he'd told her about their exchange when she'd wondered why Olivia hadn't visited.

Shaw joined her at the windows, the bitter smell of his coffee wafting over. "She doesn't hold you responsible, I hope."

"Actually, she's been more gracious than I anticipated."

"Glad to hear it."

Olivia looked at him. "You *are* going to find him?"

His expression was somber but determined. "I can't promise the result you want. I can tell you that the department wants him in custody as badly as you do. We're going to continue to work the leads."

"Thank you, Detective."

Brady strode into the room. "We're all set."

The detective shook their hands and asked Brady to reach out once he'd returned. Olivia's stomach was a bundle of nerves as they emerged from the hangar into open space. She knew her attacker couldn't have accessed the runways or surrounding fields. He hadn't followed them, either. Still, she battled a sense of impending doom.

Brady assisted her into the passenger seat and closed the door. She buckled in while he circled around the plane's nose and climbed into the pilot's seat. He glanced over at her and frowned.

"You're supposed to be less nervous this go-around." He placed his hand on her knee. "Olivia, he can't reach us here. This is a commercial airport. They have eagle eyes on the property. I checked the plane from nose to tail. She's in excellent shape."

"I know you're right."

"But my reassurances have had no effect," he murmured. His blue-gray eyes softened and roamed over her face.

His gaze zeroed in on her mouth, and her breath caught. *Be sensible. Kissing Brady will make it harder to say goodbye than it already is.*

She'd promised herself she wouldn't be irresponsible again. Doing so had ended with her married to a virtual stranger. She cared about Brady too much to repeat her mistake. He'd endured serious wounds as a child that affected his adult life. She couldn't risk inflicting more pain.

Olivia broke eye contact, and the moment was lost.

He put on his headset and engaged the intercom system so they could converse over the engine noise. "Ready?"

At her nod, he started the engine. The plane shuddered to life. "We'll let her warm up while we wait for taxi clearance."

He listened to the ATIS broadcast for information about winds and visibility. When the tower told him which runway to use, they taxied toward it. A tiny furrow between his brows was the only sign of concentration. He moved through the steps with ease. And when they were cleared for takeoff and he applied the power, working the throttle and easing back on the wheel, his mouth curved into a slight smile.

This was his safe haven, she realized. The place where his past disappeared. In the sky, Brady Johnson was comfortable with who and what he was. In the sky, far above the earth, he was free.

She surveyed the sprawling countryside below and the river's ribbons leading to the wide ocean. The patchwork of trees, fields and houses looked like a miniature train set.

The flight droned on as they left North Carolina behind and entered South Carolina air space. "There's a weather system above Myrtle Beach. I'll try to keep us above it and avoid turbulence."

He requested an increase in altitude. Outside, the blanket of wispy clouds began to thicken.

"We're doing great on fuel," he told her when they'd gained the desired altitude. "Nine gallons an hour."

She kept her focus on the sky. Suddenly, black liquid sprayed onto the windshield. "What's that?"

"Oil." He studied the instruments, his brows colliding. "The pressure's fluctuating."

"What does that mean?"

"The seals must've failed." More oil leaked out, obscuring their view.

Her heart climbed into her throat. "Meaning?"

"There's a chance the engine could shut down," he stated, his demeanor almost too casual. "I'll locate a place to land."

No engine meant an uncontrolled dive to earth, she assumed. She clutched the seat belt where it crossed her body. "How far is the nearest airport?"

"Too far." Brady consulted his GPS. "There's a patch of open land up ahead. Looks like a golf course."

She clapped her hand over her mouth.

"Liv, listen to me. This is going to be an unpleasant landing, but I've trained for this."

She projected a calm she didn't feel. "He did this, didn't he? But how? You checked everything."

His nostrils flared. "We'll figure that out later. Right now I have to concentrate on getting us on the ground without incident."

He contacted air traffic control and declared the emergency. They resolved to clear surrounding airspace.

Olivia watched the precious oil continue to spew onto the window. The plane dipped, and she screamed.

"That was me. It's okay."

She closed her eyes and began to pray.

Brady explained his intentions to air traffic control.

"How many souls on board?"

He glanced over at Olivia, who had a death grip on her seat belt. "Two people on board."

The controller alerted local emergency agencies, who'd contact the golf course. Help would be en route, should they require medical attention.

Sweat slipped beneath his collar and trickled between

his shoulder blades. He sorted through various scenarios and how he'd handle each one.

"Olivia."

"Hmm?"

"I'm going to complete a series of S-turns to bleed off altitude. That means we're going below the clouds and will encounter turbulence." He checked the forecast winds for their altitude.

She licked her lips. "Got it."

"Make sure your seat belt is snug and your shoulder harness secure." He tipped his head toward the second row of seats. "Grab that jacket. Keep it over your face when we touch down."

Fury at the man who'd sabotaged their flight simmered in his veins. This plane was in top condition. He wouldn't have taken anyone up in it, let alone Olivia, if it hadn't been. Safety protocols had been drilled into him from the day he entered Marine Corps flight school. He didn't take risks. Period. And thanks to their recent encounters, he'd taken extra time evaluating the systems before takeoff.

They flew beneath the clouds and almost instantly got hit with turbulence. The aircraft jerked and tipped. Olivia fumbled around for the sick sack. She was clearly unnerved but trying not to make a fuss.

Brady closed down the part of his mind that was set on revenge. He'd process that later.

As he executed the S-turns, he was in almost constant contact with the controller. Since wires were nearly impossible to see from above, he searched the ground for poles and buildings. He also checked the golf course flags to gauge the winds. They hit another air pocket. The fuselage rocked and jerked.

"Have you landed an airplane on a golf course before?" Olivia's subdued voice came through the headset.

"This will be a first. Fortunately, there shouldn't be any golfers out today."

"That would be a problem," she wryly exclaimed, "having to dodge caddies and golf carts."

"Brace yourself, Liv. We'll be on the ground in another five minutes. Exit the plane as soon as we come to a standstill."

Her tumultuous gaze locked onto his. The ground was rushing closer and closer. Strong winds gusted up and over the plane's body and whipped at the wings, threatening to topple the craft sideways. Their approach was far from desirable.

Just when he thought it might prove a smooth landing, the engine cut out. He didn't inform Olivia. Instead, he prayed for mercy.

With no oil supply, there was no point to attempt an engine restart. He turned off the fuel selector, along with the electrical and ignition switches, and unlatched the doors.

"Brady." She spoke his name like a warning, as if he could control their direction.

Wind pushed them too close to the trees. "Cover your face," he barked. "Hold on!"

Please, God, keep her safe.

The next second, their left wing slammed into a tree. The force spun them the opposite direction. The world outside the windows blurred. The screech of ripping metal pierced his eardrums. Another tree stopped their motion with a jarring halt. The smell of leaking gasoline filled the plane. Through it all, Olivia didn't make a sound.

TWENTY

"Olivia?" He reached for the jacket obscuring her head.

He removed it and found her slumped over, her eyes closed.

"Liv, honey, wake up."

The stench of gasoline permeated the fuselage. They had to get out before fire erupted.

He gently jostled her shoulder. "Liv? Can you hear me?"

She moaned. Her eyelids fluttered.

He searched for visible injuries and checked her pulse.

"We didn't land in the treetops, did we?" she murmured, lifting her hand and probing her forehead.

"We're on solid ground. Come on, let's get out of here." He tried to convey urgency without alarming her. If a fire broke out, they'd have minutes to escape.

Olivia's door wouldn't budge. "The tree's wedged it closed." She tried again, applying force with her shoulder and leaning her whole body into it. She thumped it with her fist. "Useless."

Brady's opened, but there wasn't enough space for either of them to fit through.

Sirens announced the approach of welcome assistance. But how long until they reached them?

Her dark eyes assessed him. "What now?"

He wrapped the jacket around his arm and, climbing into the back seat, began beating at the plexiglass window. After several repeated blows, Olivia joined him. She lifted her cast.

"Let me try."

"And risk reinjuring your arm?"

"I smell the gasoline, Brady. And I see the worry in your eyes."

Taking the jacket and wrapping it around her cast, she nudged him aside and started hammering at a spot by the window seal. That area was weakened by damage and, after multiple repeated blows, began to give way. Brady told her to rest. He flipped his body and used his feet to kick out the window. He scrambled through the opening, slid down and assisted her to safety.

By the time he and Olivia managed to get free of the accident site, EMTs were on the scene. After he and Olivia were assessed, they waited off to the side as officials discussed the best plan of action.

Olivia folded her hand into his. "It's a total loss, isn't it?"

He dragged his gaze from the wreckage. A halo of fine tendrils had escaped her braid, and dirt smudged her cheek. "It can be replaced."

Her forehead puckered, and a protest formed on her lips.

"We're safe." Cupping her cheek, he gently thumbed the dirt from her skin. "That's the only thing that matters."

"Thanks to your skills and quick thinking." She captured his hand, brought it to her mouth and brushed her lips over his knuckles.

A shock wave shuddered through him. When she pressed his hand to her cheek, her molten brown eyes full of gratitude and something akin to longing, his knees went weak. Logic had no role in this equation. If there weren't witnesses around, he'd pull her into his arms and kiss her soundly.

But they weren't alone. Although it was for the best, he couldn't help but regret the others' presence.

A law enforcement officer drove them to a rental car company, where Brady secured a sedan. They'd been able to recover most of Olivia's belongings from the wreckage. They stored everything in the car's trunk and sought out a secluded booth in a hotel restaurant. The lunch rush had already passed, granting them privacy. One couple conversed over salads at the bar, and a family of four occupied one of the booths by the bank of windows. The lone server took their orders and returned to the kitchen.

Across the table, Olivia toyed with her straw, stabbing at the lemon and jostling the ice cubes. "What now?"

"That's up to you." Brady had been against her plan to go off on her own. If anything, today's accident reinforced his stance. "We can drive to Charleston or return to Jacksonville. Or we can rent a couple of rooms and sleep on it. Decide what to do in the morning."

Her mouth was an unhappy line. "We don't know for sure whether or not my attacker is responsible for what happened."

"I've been reviewing everything I did during preflight. Nothing stood out to me. The only thing I can think of that could've caused the oil loss is a blocked crankshaft breather tube." At her blank look, he explained. "The tube is meant to rid the engine of water vapor and any liquid water. If there's blockage, the engine pressurizes and causes the seals to fail. The oil leaks out and the engine shuts down."

"The engine didn't shut down, though."

He lowered his gaze and rubbed at the condensation on his glass. She slapped the table with her palm.

"Are you serious? We lost engine power during flight, and you didn't tell me?"

"It happened upon approach. Late in the game. It didn't make sense to upset you."

She flopped against the booth and shook her head. "Upset me any more than I already was? Not possible."

"You did great, Liv. You held it together like a seasoned flier." His phone rang. "It's Detective Shaw."

They'd spoken to him during the ride to the rental company.

Brady set it to speaker so Olivia could listen in. "One of the airport employees, Trent Sanders, didn't report for work last week. His boss assumed he'd quit without notice. When Officer Whaley went out to his apartment to interview him, he discovered his door ajar. Mr. Sanders's body was in the kitchen. Killed with a bullet between his eyes."

Olivia gasped. "That's horrible."

"He worked in the office and had access to the light aircraft," Shaw continued. "He's supposed to have a pair of airport uniforms. We've only been able to locate one. Our theory is our guy followed Sanders home, killed him, and used his uniform and ID card to access the hangar."

"Only a handful of people were aware of our travel plans," Brady said.

"You took Olivia on a flight recently, did you not?"

He'd flown her to the beach for a day, an outing he'd enjoyed far more than he should've, given the circumstances. "Yes."

"He probably assumed you'd take her up again eventually. It was his plan B."

Their food arrived. When the server was out of earshot, he said, "I assume you're going over the security footage?"

"I'm driving to the airport now to do just that."

Olivia snorted. "He's been a pro at avoiding them so far."

"He's familiar with the aquarium," Shaw pointed out.

"This feels like a spur-of-the-moment decision. He's growing weary of the game. Let's hope that means he's not as meticulous as he usually is."

After they disconnected, they ate their food without much enthusiasm.

She picked up another fry and let it dangle from her fingertips. "If our assumption that he's prior military is right, then he must've worked around planes."

He wiped his mouth with his napkin. "That tube is in a hard-to-reach area. A blockage can easily be overlooked. I replaced the old one last year with the kind with a slit already in place in case of buildup. He would've had to insert the obstruction above the slit to have the desired effect." He texted Shaw. "The aquarium vet was a sniper. Let's see if he also worked around planes."

"You still suspect Zach?"

"I'll put it this way—I have no reason to clear him just yet."

When their bill had been paid, they made their way through the lobby. Brady's phone rang again. He took Olivia's hand and tugged her into an alcove made private with artificial plants and overstuffed chairs.

Shaw was on video chat this time. There was no denying his mood had improved.

"We have an image."

Olivia clapped her hands together.

"It's not perfect," he cautioned. "A ball cap obscured most of his face, but we can see his height and build."

"That's a start," Brady said.

"Olivia, I'd like for you to return to Jacksonville and study this image. There may be some detail about him that's significant to you."

She squared her shoulders. "All right."

"Good. You guys be careful on the roads. They're calling for a decrease in temperatures throughout the day and possible ice overnight."

Brady didn't try to mask his relief. "We should be there by supper time. See you soon."

She arched a brow. "I could've looked at the image on my phone."

"Shaw wants you on hand to help with any breaks in the case. What if he needs you to pick someone out of a lineup?"

"You don't have to look so pleased, you know."

"Admit it, Liv. You're happy."

"And why would that be?"

"Because." He grinned at her. "You would've missed me too much."

Considering the day she'd had, Olivia wanted nothing more than to hide beneath her bedcovers. The airplane scare had been followed by a long drive up the coast. At the police station, they'd studied the grainy surveillance photo in vain. The image had offered scant clues. Afterward, instead of going straight to Brady's, they'd had to divert to the aquarium. Ruth had called and insisted Olivia sign documents absolving the aquarium of any wrongdoing.

"I didn't think I'd be back here so soon."

The contrast between the freezing air outside and the aquarium's balmy interior was enough to stop her in her tracks. Olivia paused inside the main entrance and soaked in the familiar sights and sounds. Thanks to the worsening weather conditions, most of the guests had left. Only half an hour remained of the business day, anyway.

Brady trailed his fingers down the middle of her back. "This will all blow over eventually, and you will reclaim your good memories."

"This is my second home, yet a stranger's vendetta could force me to walk away forever. I wish I'd been able to identify the man in the video footage."

"We know more than we did before. Caucasian male in his twenties or thirties. Medium build."

"But no identifying markers."

"They're still processing the airport employee's apartment and interviewing neighbors."

"I pray they get this guy before anyone else gets hurt."

The director greeted them and motioned to the chairs in front of her desk. "I'm sorry to call you in on a day like this, but the powers that be want to cover their bases." Her laugh had a nervous trill to it.

"I've already indicated I won't sue the aquarium."

"They don't want any nasty surprises later on." Pushing the papers across the desk, she nudged the pen holder.

Olivia noticed a sheen of perspiration on Ruth's face. She looked flushed, as well.

"Ruth, are you feeling all right?"

She touched the locket necklace around her throat. "A-As a matter of fact, I suspect I'm coming down with something." She stared at the leaden skies visible through the windows. "I'd planned on staying overnight in case of a power outage. The last time we had an ice storm, we lost power for twelve hours."

Brady had opted to remain standing by the door. "What happens to the animals in that scenario?"

"We have backup generators that will keep their systems running."

Olivia twisted in her chair. "It's common practice to keep a small number of employees on-site during uncertain weather events. Someone has to handle feedings and other issues that may arise."

"It's early in the season for snow, let alone ice."

"We've had mild winters in recent years," Ruth interjected. "We're overdue."

Olivia read the statement peppered with legal jargon and signed her name. She dropped the pen into the holder and stood. "There, that should make them happy."

Ruth put her name down as a witness. She braced her hands on the table and pushed to her feet. "Your absence has been felt throughout the aquarium, Olivia." Taking a tissue from its box, she patted her forehead dry.

"Ruth, you should go home. Or better yet, a clinic. You don't look well."

Her professional, unruffled demeanor slipped, and for a split second, she looked as if she might break down in tears. Her gaze fell to her desk, however, and she stiffened her spine. "I'll think on it. Be careful getting home."

Brady's expression bordered on suspicious. Nearing the escalator, he said, "Something's off. She seemed more anxious than unwell."

"I haven't ever seen her like that," she agreed.

As they descended the escalator, she spotted Maya near the sturgeon petting area.

The younger woman didn't notice them at first. Her shoulders hunched, she dashed tears from her cheeks and wiped her palms over her pants.

"Maya?"

"Olivia." Her eyes widened. "I didn't expect to see you here."

"Ruth asked me to come in. How have you been?"

"Not good." Fresh tears welled. "I should've listened to you."

Olivia shared a glance with Brady. "What's wrong?"

"It's Bruno. He's bad news, like you said. I found out he did something terrible." Guilt danced over her features. "I ended things. He was angry."

Brady stepped closer. "Do you have reason to believe he'd hurt you?"

She hooked her hair behind her ears. "It's not me I'm worried about."

Apprehension washed over her. Was she the person Maya was worried about? "Maya, you should tell the police what you know."

"I don't know anything." Her gaze skittered away, and she backed up. "I have to go."

"Maya, wait—"

Ruth rushed into the atrium and called Olivia's name. She turned around, and Maya dashed outside.

"Detective Shaw's theory about her boyfriend is looking more likely," Brady said in a low voice. "She smacked of guilt and regret. Maybe the person he hurt is you."

"As soon as we're done here, we should call him. Maya could be in danger simply for kicking him to the curb. He doesn't sound like a humble guy."

"Not to mention she has dirt on him."

Ruth reached them then. "Olivia, I'm glad I caught you. I've decided to take your advice and see a doctor." She had her purse hooked over her shoulder, her keys in one hand. "I don't feel comfortable leaving the aquarium in Don Welch's supervision. He's an adept security head, but his knowledge doesn't extend to the animals. James isn't answering his phone. I hate to ask, but would you be willing to oversee operations until I can get back?"

Brady shook his head, silently urging her to decline. She shrugged. How could she say no? "Of course, I'll do it."

"Olivia—"

"Don is here," she assured him. "It's only for a few hours. I'll ask Jacksonville PD if they could spare an officer."

Ruth surprised Olivia with a hug. "You're a good person." Spinning away, she rushed outside. Through the glass, they saw her turn and stare at them, her mouth a troubled line. She offered a half-hearted wave and left.

"I have a bad feeling about this." Brady pinched the bridge of his nose.

Olivia didn't want to admit Ruth's behavior unnerved her. "We'll call Shaw and relay our concerns about both women."

He nodded to the scene outside. An icy drizzle made patterns on the sidewalk. A layer of ice on the road would make travel impossible, and buildup on tree limbs would impact power lines. "Ruth may not be able to return, even if she wants to." His blue-gray gaze was stormy. "We may be stuck here for the night."

TWENTY-ONE

"Let's meet up with Don and find out who else is staying," Olivia said. "It would be easier than touring the twin buildings and possibly missing someone."

Brady fell into step beside her. His gut instincts were screaming to get her out of there. Maya had hinted at trouble that might involve Olivia, and the director had spooked him with that strange stare. He also didn't like that the department hadn't been able to spare an officer. The weather was worsening, and they needed all staff on hand to help with potential emergencies.

"Later, we'll raid the snack bar." She nudged his side. "I know for a fact there are orange-and-vanilla popsicles."

He couldn't summon much enthusiasm. He'd pictured them secure inside his house, eating ice cream on his comfortable couch and watching mindless television. After having to deal with a forced landing and then a lengthy drive from Charleston, Brady was feeling the punch of fatigue.

She sensed his lingering dismay. "Once we've taken care of the evening feedings, we'll either hang out in my office or the employee break room. No more roaming."

"I understand why you agreed to this." Not only was she devoted to the animals' well-being, but she was also a selfless person. "I just wish Ruth hadn't put you on the spot."

"She didn't choose to become ill."

"That depends on how good of an actress she is," he muttered.

Olivia fell silent. They used one of the employee stairwells to reach the basement. Emerging into the cavernous area, she put her hand out. Raised voices bounced off the thick walls.

"That sounds like Roman," she said quietly.

They walked slowly past the pumps and around the corner, where Roman was arguing with a stranger.

Her brow puckered. "I wonder what that's about."

Roman grabbed the other man by the throat and shoved him against the wall.

Brady stiffened. "Nothing good. Do you recognize that man?"

"He's wearing the salt-company uniform. He must be the delivery driver. What would Roman want with him?"

"Let's ask."

The pair belatedly noticed their approach and broke apart.

"Olivia." Roman's expression was inscrutable. "What are you doing down here?"

"Ruth had to leave, and she asked me to stay in her place." She looked pointedly at the driver, who found something interesting in the floor. "What's going on?"

"A misunderstanding, that's all." Roman gestured to the other man. "You were leaving, weren't you?"

The driver smoothed the front of his shirt and nodded. When he passed between Olivia and Brady, she tensed.

Brady noticed her reaction. His brows lifted in unspoken question.

She cleared her throat. "Are you staying overnight, Roman?"

"Me? You know that's not my cup of tea. I'm going

to fetch something from my locker before I go." Roman speared Brady with a sharp stare. "Enjoy yourselves."

They watched him leave via a wide hallway.

Olivia seized his wrist. "When the driver walked by me, I was hit with the overwhelming smell of brine and seawater. He smelled exactly like the trunk I was almost stuffed inside. We have to follow him."

The sound of a clanging metal door led them to a delivery area with oversize garage-style doors. They broke into a run. By the time they pushed open the door, he was inside his delivery truck and revving the engine. When Olivia started to go after him, Brady caught her hand.

"Wait."

"Why?"

"He could have a weapon."

"You're armed."

"I can't fire on a guy based on how he smells. We need more proof than that. If he suspects we're onto him and manages to get away, he'll destroy any evidence."

She reluctantly agreed. Brady's call to Detective Shaw went to voice mail.

"Read off the license plate number. I'll text him the info."

Olivia rattled it off. The wind shifted and pushed rain into the covered area. Brady pocketed his phone and ushered her inside.

"He didn't act like he was nursing a gunshot wound," she mused, folding her arms over herself and chafing her upper arms.

"I might've only clipped him. That would be relatively easy to hide."

"Do you think it's him?"

He recognized her desperation, because he was nearing the end of his rope, too. "He fits the description. Hold on, did you notice Roman looked different?"

"What do you mean?"

"He shaved. The man in the video image was clean-shaven."

Her face scrunched. "Roman? He's grumpy and abrupt, I'll grant you that. I haven't seen him lose his temper until today. But is he capable of pulling off elaborate murder attempts?"

"Maybe he's working with the salt-truck driver. Has he shaved his beard since he's been here?"

"No."

"Let's have another talk with him."

"All right."

On the first floor, they were waylaid by the head of security.

"Don, have you seen Roman?"

"I just let him out the main entrance."

Olivia planted her hands on her hips. "He said he had to retrieve something from his locker."

Don shrugged, his hooded gaze sliding between them. "Must've changed his mind."

"Who else is staying tonight?"

"Becky Colburn and Tim Woods. They're in the other building. I'm headed down to the office, in case you need me." Don scowled at the glazed sidewalk visible through the wall of glass. "Freezing rain. Won't be too long before the streets will be impassable."

When he'd gone, Olivia sent Brady an apologetic look. "You were right. Even if Ruth or James could get back here, it wouldn't be safe for us to try and navigate slick roads."

"We'll make the best of it."

The next two hours were spent doling out the evening

feedings. Afterward, Olivia led the way to the snack bar. She heated up corn dogs and giant slices of pizza and told him to raid the ice cream cooler. They left cash in the drawer to cover the cost and carried their bounty upstairs to the employee break room.

"I haven't eaten like this since flight school," he said, taking a moment to lock the door behind them.

She laughed. "This is what people do when they're stranded by foul weather."

She tuned the television to a local station and joined him at one of the tables. They listened to the weather report while they ate.

"I remember one particularly bad winter in Cherokee. We had freezing rain off and on for days, which resulted in the loss of electricity. It wasn't restored for two weeks in some areas. Of course, the kids didn't mind. We didn't have to go to school."

The door knob rattled, and she jerked. Brady stood up, tipping his chair back in the process. Through the glass, they could see a woman with very short brown hair and dangly earrings.

"It's Becky."

Olivia unlocked the door. The other employee, Tim, was with her. They had come in search of food.

"There's plenty here," Olivia said. "Please join us."

After introductions were made, the pair settled in and conversation turned to aquarium affairs. Brady couldn't help but notice Olivia's enthusiasm for the topic. He hated that she'd been deprived of her life's chosen work.

It was ten o'clock when Tim retreated to his office for the night. He'd brought a sleeping bag and pillow, as had Becky.

"We weren't planning to stay the night, so we're ill prepared." Olivia cleared the last of the garbage and placed it in the receptacle.

"Isn't there extra bedding in the room off the auditorium?" Becky said, yawning.

"I forgot." She turned to Brady. "We store sleeping bags there in case our Sleep with the Sharks guests need it."

"Tell me where it is, exactly, and I'll fetch it."

"It'll be easier to come with you."

Becky bid them good-night and shuffled to her office. As they set out on their errand, Shaw texted.

"He pulled up the salt truck plates and, with a single phone call, got the driver's name. Merlin Hunley. He has a squeaky-clean record, it appears."

Her shoulders slumped. "Another dead end."

He settled his hand on her nape and massaged the taut muscles. "He's promised to keep digging. They're currently processing the fingerprints from the dead employee's apartment. That may turn up something useful."

"I suppose." Olivia tugged open the auditorium door, and they started to descend the steep steps. Moments later, the lights flickered out. The room was plunged into inky darkness.

Her fingers reached back and tangled with his. "There goes the electricity."

"What about the generators?"

"They emit enough power to run the pumping system and illuminate the exits. That's about it."

He activated his phone's flashlight. The beam hardly penetrated the vast space around them. They retrieved the sleeping bags and blankets and retraced their steps. Out in the atrium, the tanks' humming filled the space. The exit signs glared red. Beyond the glass walls, the streets were unlit, the buildings a network of mysterious shapes.

The gunshot came out of nowhere. Pain exploded in Brady's lower leg.

He lunged for Olivia, determined to shield her.

Brady's arms closed around her, and he maneuvered her back inside the auditorium.

Another bullet struck the thick door.

"We have to move," he grunted, tugging her toward the stairs. "I dropped my phone out there."

She grabbed his hand. "This way."

Picturing the space in her mind, she led him to the left side and used the paneled wall to guide them down. They were almost to the bottom when she heard the door creak open. Another shot blasted through the room. Her fingers tightening on Brady's, she lurched through the door first.

He closed and locked it behind him. She noticed he was breathing heavily but put it down to the chase.

"Through here," she instructed, grateful she knew these rooms' layouts like the back of her hand. "When we exit, we can either take the basement corridor to the other building or go up the escalator and try to reach Don's office."

He didn't immediately answer. She forged ahead, holding tightly to his hand. When they emerged, he left the decision up to her.

"Basement it is," she murmured, praying she was right.

A single light pierced the gloom of the dank underground tunnel. They raced through it, desperate to reach the other building and find a place to hide long enough to contact Don. Olivia noticed Brady was slowing.

"What's the matter?" She could barely make out his features.

Before he could answer, footsteps striking the cement floor alerted them that the shooter was in pursuit.

Inside the other building, he sagged against the wall and doubled over. Alarmed, she edged close.

"Brady?"

"I'm fine." Gulping in air, he shoved upright. "Where to?"

"Are you hurt?"

"It's nothing." He folded his fingers through hers. "You're in charge here. Where do we go?"

"We can barricade ourselves in the scuba equipment room."

"Lead the way."

Olivia tried not to think about the weakness in his voice. There was no time to demand answers. She avoided the obvious route—the unmoving escalator where she'd been pushed—and led him through a series of stairways and halls until they reached the shark tank area. It was the closest route to the scuba equipment room.

She locked the door and, pulling him farther into the room, flicked on her phone light and scanned him from head to toe. Blood stained his right pants leg below the knee.

"You got shot?" she cried out. "Why didn't you tell me?"

He sank onto a metal bench. "Wasn't time."

"Don't move. I'll get the first aid kit."

Olivia ignored his protests. She grabbed the kit from the nearby office and raced back. Her fingers were shaking as she handed him the phone.

"Hold this."

"Liv, it can wait—"

"No, it can't."

He sighed and aimed the flashlight. She rolled up his pants leg and bit down hard on her inner cheek when she glimpsed the torn, bloody flesh. She made a mess of the contents as she searched for a pad and gauze.

"Don't worry about antibiotic cream," he said in a controlled voice. "Just wrap it up."

"And if the bullet's still in there?"

"It can be dug out later."

She got the wound covered with a snug wrapping of gauze. "Let's pray that stems the bleeding."

"Your prayers won't help you," snarled a voice behind them.

Olivia whirled around. The single light in the hallway illuminated his features from above, distorting them. "Roman?" Shock immobilized her. "It was you all along?"

Brady slowly stood and used his body to block her.

"The police are on their way," Brady said, bluffing. "You don't want to add two more homicides to your list of crimes, do you?"

He sneered. "Where I come from, there are people who can make that all go away."

"Where you're from? You mean New Jersey?" she demanded.

His eyes narrowed, and he took a step closer. "So it's true. Matteo told you who he really was."

"Derek told me nothing. I found out after his death. What I don't understand is why his family wants me dead. Why send you here to infiltrate my life?"

"My job was to ferret out what secrets Matteo shared with you—"

"He didn't tell me anything," she asserted. "Don't you see? Derek buried Matteo Giordano and had no plans to resurrect him."

"You should've been more up-front about your relationship. If you'd convinced me of your blissful ignorance, maybe I wouldn't have to kill you."

"Since when did we have heart-to-hearts?"

"What's your connection with the salt-truck driver?" Brady inched forward.

"None of your business."

"Did you pay him to do your dirty work?" He continued to advance. Olivia snagged his shirt, but he kept going. "Was that him out in the woods? Tell me, which one of you did I clip?"

"That coward?" He gave a bark of laughter. "Merlin's the skittish sort. I had to twist his arm to get him to look the other way."

"You convinced him to do what? Help you avoid the security cameras?"

Roman noticed how close Brady had gotten. "Stop right there."

Brady obeyed and held up his hands. "I'm just trying to get answers. Ruth was acting twitchy. Did you have a role in her summons of Olivia?"

He smiled and shrugged. "Some people are easy to manipulate."

"She wasn't physically sick," Olivia surmised. "She was sick with guilt over what you'd made her do."

The gun was pointed at Brady's chest. One twitch of Roman's finger, and Brady was a dead man. Olivia couldn't bear to stand by and do nothing.

"I'm not going to make this easy for you," she yelled, sprinting toward the walkway suspended above the tank.

Please, please let him come after me and leave Brady alone.

"You want me, Roman?" she taunted over her shoulder. "Come and get me!"

"Olivia!" Horror painted Brady's voice.

As she pounded across the walkway, she heard a scuffle behind her. She twisted around and saw the men struggling for control of the gun. Roman landed a kick against

Brady's wounded calf. It gave the monster a couple of seconds' headway. Roman leaped onto the bridge and shot at her.

The bullet missed by inches.

She ran faster. The distance across to the other side seemed impossibly long. The walkway vibrated and swayed. Below them, the water was an opaque abyss.

Brady recovered and raced after them. With a growl, Roman turned back and charged.

Olivia screamed a warning.

The men collided. Roman used Brady's wound to gain the upper hand.

She made the decision to retrace her steps. Before she could reach them, Roman managed to shove Brady over the edge.

Time slowed as he hit the water and disappeared beneath the surface.

TWENTY-TWO

Olivia scrambled to the railing. "Brady!"

She started to climb over. Roman grabbed a fistful of her hair and yanked her back.

"He's shark bait."

"No," she gasped, attempting to free herself.

"They may be fed on a regular schedule, but once they get a whiff of his blood…well, I don't envy the employee who discovers the remains of your brave captain."

Roman shoved the gun into her ribs and propelled her off the walkway and through the tank room. Terror enveloped her in a black haze. She couldn't think straight. Brady couldn't die. She couldn't lose him. He meant too much. He meant *everything*.

How could she not have recognized what was happening? She'd tried to be careful with her heart. She'd failed spectacularly.

"Move it," he growled, shoving her through the door.

Now there was a good chance they wouldn't make it out of here alive.

Stay calm, Brady repeated in his head. *Don't panic.*

The tank was an unlit abyss beneath him. He wished he'd never watched *Jaws*. Where were the sharks?

He forced himself to push through the water with slow precision when he was desperate to locate the diving platform and find Olivia.

Something brushed his foot. He jerked away, expecting razor-sharp teeth to sink into his already mangled calf muscle.

Where was the platform?

Where was Olivia?

I didn't mean to, Derek, but I fell for her. She's the most amazing woman I've ever met.

The water rippled off to his right. He had to focus. No telling how much blood he'd lost. He couldn't afford to lose consciousness in here.

He found the wall, but it was slippery. No place to grab hold.

Fighting increasing alarm, he treaded water and tried to get his bearings.

His gaze followed the walkway. The darkness swallowed up both ends. Which way to the tank entrance?

There was a sound, like a motor revving, and the lights blinked on.

Brady almost wished they hadn't.

Only a few feet away was the largest shark in the tank. Rows of jagged teeth were clearly visible. He held his breath, stopped treading, and attempted to grip the wall and keep from sliding down.

The massive animal moved at a snail's pace through the water.

Just when Brady thought the predator was uninterested, he turned his head and changed direction. He was coming straight for him.

"You don't have to do this." Olivia was getting desperate. Roman had forced her into the tunnel, and now they were in the other building, nearing the topmost landing. "You can lock me in a closet and leave. Go back to New Jersey. Your bosses will make sure you aren't found."

"My bosses will bury me in cement if I don't carry out their orders. It's either you or me." He pushed her against the railing and put distance between them. The gun was aimed at her chest. "You've made a mess of things, you know that? If you'd suffocated at the bottom of the tank like I'd intended, I could've continued my lucrative side business."

"What business?"

"Diamonds. Do you know how easy it is to hide them in the salt sacks?"

"That's why you needed Merlin?"

"I also hid gems in the merchandise, but that was too unpredictable."

"The shipment of stuffed animals that went missing. That was you."

"This gig pays me triple what the Giordanos pay." He scowled. "I'm going to have to abandon it, thanks to you and your boyfriend. The heat will be on once they find your bodies. Now, climb over the railing."

Olivia glanced behind her and shuddered. The ground floor was four stories below. She'd never survive.

"Tell me something first. How did you expect to pass yourself off as an educated aquarist?"

"Easy. I am an educated aquarist. I didn't go to college. I got hands-on training in my parents' pet store. I was in charge of the aquatic side of things. That's why the family chose me."

"How did you know what to do to sabotage Brady's plane?"

"You forget. I'm in the killing business." He motioned with his gun. "No more stalling. Climb over."

"Roman, please. Have you no conscience? No heart?" He'd acted genuinely concerned about her broken arm.

He'd brazenly signed his name on her cast, knowing full well he'd inflicted her injuries. Sick.

"Not anymore."

He motioned with his gun. "Now do as I said."

Her entire body trembling, she climbed over and planted her feet on the slim ledge.

"Good girl. Any last words before you jump?"

The outright evil in the man she'd worked alongside gutted her. She glanced at the closest set of stairs. If she could reach them, she could possibly scale over and around.

"Don't even think about it." He began to stalk over.

"Stop right there!"

Olivia's mouth went dry. A soggy, bedraggled Brady had entered from the turtle gallery.

Roman spun and fired.

Brady returned fire, striking Roman in the hand. He yelped and, his face twisting with fury, lunged for Olivia. He repeatedly slammed his fist on her fingers where she gripped the railing.

She yanked one hand away to escape the onslaught. A scream ripped from her lips as her feet slipped from the ledge. Her body dangled above the cavernous space. She made the mistake of looking down. The cement floor would break every bone in her body if she plummeted from this height.

Brady tackled Roman from behind and ripped him off the railing.

Olivia's hands were slick with sweat. She called on all of her strength to regain her balance and grip.

The crack of the gun butt against Roman's skull resounded, and his knees failed. He slumped to the floor, nearly taking Brady with him.

"Hold on, sweetheart," Brady called. Running over, he seized her around the waist and hauled her over.

Hugging her close, he walked her away from the edge. He ran his hands over her hair. "You're okay," he murmured, kissing the top of her head. "Thank the Lord, you're okay."

Tears streaming down her cheeks, she burrowed into his chest. "Oh, Brady, I thought I'd lost you forever. And then he ordered me to jump… I thought it was the end."

He cradled her face and kissed her hard and fast. "Let's get him restrained before he comes to."

Crouching down, Brady worked Roman's leather belt free and strapped his wrists together.

"Where did you get the gun?" She picked it up and handed it over.

"Don Welch." He tucked the weapon into his waistband and snagged Roman's, as well. "He helped me out of the tank and gave it to me. The funny thing is, he vanished after that. I have no idea where he went."

"That's strange."

"He could've gone to check on Becky and Tim."

"The police may not be able to get here quickly." She pointed to Roman's prone form. "What will we do with him?"

"Put him in a secure holding room, preferably without makeshift weapons on the off chance he manages to get free."

"The storage room he locked us in has nothing but papers and lost-and-found clothing."

Brady gave her a grim smile. "I like the way you think."

Together, they lugged him into the service elevator and got him into the storage closet. She took the master set of keys from his belt loop and locked him inside. They left him only long enough to rouse Becky and Tim—both unharmed—and contact the authorities. Part of Olivia feared he wouldn't be where they'd left him. But they heard him pounding on the door and shouting obscenities.

"We were wrong about Bruno being involved," she said. "And Zach."

"Maya should still steer clear of him."

"I'll try to convince her of the wisdom of that, but I'm not sure she'll listen."

"I believe she knows she messed up. And that you care about her."

Brady took her hand and motioned to the opposite side of the room, in sight of the closet but far enough to be spared the racket. He sat on the floor and patted the spot beside him. When she was settled, he put his arm around her and pulled her close.

She rested her head on his shoulder. "For the first time in weeks, I feel like I can breathe normally."

"I don't know about you, but I could use a real vacation."

Lifting her head, she angled her face toward his. "What if the Giordanos send someone else to finish what Roman started?"

"Shaw will offer Roman a deal. He gives up enough information to put the key members of their family behind bars, he gets a lighter sentence. Besides, they'll figure out you're not a threat. If you had dirt on them, this would be the time to share. Your continued silence will be proof of that." His arm tightened around her. "I will be by your side every day until I'm confident the danger has passed."

"And after that?" she murmured, her heart racing. "We go our separate ways?"

"No." His hand curved around her cheek. "I couldn't bear that."

His lips covered hers, sweet and searching. There was a reverence in the way he held her, as if afraid she'd vanish into thin air.

She caressed his jaw. "I like you, Brady."

He tensed. "I'm glad to hear that," he said carefully.

Sliding her other hand around his neck, she said, "I also respect and admire you."

His blue-gray gaze delved into hers, probing and questioning. Hoping. "That, too."

"I trust you." The corners of his mouth turned down. She smiled. "There's more to it, though. My heart yearns for you. Belongs to you, actually, whether you want it or not. Brady, there will never be another man for me."

His throat worked. "Are you saying what I think you're saying?"

"I love you."

He closed his eyes and, with a ragged sigh, buried his face in the curve of her neck and hugged her close. "I love you, Liv."

God had blessed them both with an unlooked-for love, one that would stand the test of time. She understood now that what she'd had with Derek had been akin to fool's gold—bright, sparkly and alluring on the outside, but cheap and false where it counted. Brady was a man of honor, a man who, because of his loss and pain, would cherish his loved ones. With God's help, she would strive to show him unconditional love, every day they were gifted together.

EPILOGUE

Brady was conversing with Olivia's uncle when she approached from behind and looped her arms around him.

"Come with me to the waterfall?" She kissed the side of his neck.

He latched onto her hands and pulled her more firmly against him.

"Is there a specific reason you want me all to yourself?" he teased.

"Do I need one?"

He chuckled. "You already know the answer to that."

Making his excuses to her uncle, he left the picnic table and threaded his fingers through hers. They picked their way through the crowd of relatives and friends, side-stepping blankets thrown over the grass and dodging the ball being kicked among a group of kids. A light breeze tweaked the tree leaves, relieving the late August heat.

"Where do you think you're off to?" Julian teased. He and Audrey sat in matching lawn chairs, their hands linked midair between them. After more than a year of marriage, they still acted like newlyweds.

"None of your business," Brady shot back, unable to keep from grinning.

Olivia's laughter further buoyed his spirits. She'd been tired lately and distracted, which wasn't like her. He'd worried something was wrong at the aquarium. Immediately after Roman's arrest, Ruth had confessed that he'd coerced her to summon Olivia to the aquarium that night. Although she'd done it to protect her family, she'd resigned. It had taken months to hire a new director, and Olivia had indicated it had been a rocky transition. Erin had returned to work eventually, and she'd even asked Olivia to be a bridesmaid in her wedding. Maya had gotten wise and cut Bruno and his buddies out of her life. She was taking her job seriously and had even come to church with Brady and Olivia on several occasions.

Don Welch was in prison for his role in the attacks. He'd taken bribes from Roman but, in the end, hadn't had the stomach for murder. He'd given Brady a weapon that final night and taken off. The police had found him at his ex-wife's house. Roman's trial was over, and he'd be spending a significant portion of his life behind bars. His testimony helped put away key members of the Giordano family, which meant he and Olivia didn't have to worry about further threats. She'd even exchanged letters with Derek's mother and sister. Both women were sorry for Olivia's troubles and grateful to learn about Derek's life after he left them.

Today there was no sign of fatigue. She was radiant. The feminine pink blouse accentuated her tan skin, dark eyes and jet-black hair.

"Did I thank you yet for organizing this surprise?" he said.

"Only a dozen times." Her eyes shone with affection.

"I'll thank you a dozen more."

He paused to observe the festivities. The pavilions were decorated with balloons and streamers. People sampled the vast array of dishes, cooked up by Olivia's aunts and grandmothers. Games of cornhole and horseshoes were set up in the shade of giant oaks.

They'd come to the Qualla Boundary, the land trust owned by the Eastern Band of Cherokee Indians, ostensibly for a casual family visit. He'd grown fond of her family, especially her mom and sisters. They'd been cautious in the beginning, after what had happened with Derek, and had appreciated that he hadn't rushed things. He and Olivia had waited a year to tie the knot in a sentimental, beautiful Christmas ceremony.

"Seriously, Olivia. This is the best birthday celebration I've ever had. I don't believe you'll be able to top it."

Her slow smile challenged him. "We'll see."

She'd even managed to arrange for his other friends, Cade and Tori, to fly in from California. He could see the couple strolling side by side on the periphery, their toddler son riding on Cade's shoulders. Cat had been invited, but work obligations had prevented her.

Together, they climbed the trail along the tree line. The sound of splashing water reached them before they emerged into a clearing.

"It's stunning," he said, admiring nature's beauty.

"This was one of my favorite places to come as a kid."

"I'm glad you brought me here."

"I have one last present for you." She produced a small package.

"You've already given me so much," he said, his chest growing tight.

"Go ahead, open it."

He unwrapped the fragile paper. Inside, there was a small white roll of fabric. "What is it? Handkerchiefs? A special cloth to polish my new airplane?"

"Unroll it."

He unfurled the soft material and stared. "It's a T-shirt. An impossibly tiny T-shirt with snaps."

Shaking her head, she took it from him and flipped it over. World's Greatest Dad. The printed words didn't register, at first. "Wait," he said, his heart thundering against his ribs. "Wait."

"Brady, you're going to be a father." Her eyes were soft with love and dreams fulfilled. "We're going to have a baby."

He could hardly speak. "When?"

"I'm three months along. Don't worry, I've been to see the doctor. Everything is normal. You can come with me for the first ultrasound, if you want."

Brady leaned against a nearby tree and ran his fingers over the outfit. He imagined a living, breathing infant wearing it. His and Olivia's child. Moisture filled his eyes.

"I've shocked you," she said, her hands twisting at her waist.

"Yes, you have."

She frowned.

He held out his hand and, when she'd grasped it, eased her close. He settled his other hand low on her stomach. Wonder filled him.

"I thought you couldn't make me happier. I was mistaken."

He met her lips in a lingering, heartfelt kiss.

"You're going to be a fantastic mother," he told her. "I'll make you a promise, Liv. You and our baby. I will seek God's wisdom and strength every day. I want to be a good husband and father."

"You already are a good husband," she vowed, beaming. "As for the father part, there are no doubts in my mind."

"I don't have an example to pattern myself after."

"But you know what *not* to do. You know what a child needs and craves. Besides, the time you spend with Michael and the others is invaluable practice."

"Have I told you lately how much I love you, Mrs. Johnson?"

"Tell me again, Mr. Johnson." She lifted her face to his. "Better yet, show me."

* * * * *

Dear Reader,

The idea for this book's setting came to me last year, when I had the opportunity to accompany my son on an overnight field trip to a local aquarium. There was something mysterious and exciting about being there after hours. I'll never forget spending the night in the shark tunnel, watching the sharks and fish swim overhead as I drifted off to sleep. I shared my idea with our aquarium guide that night, and she agreed it would be a unique setting. I'm sure she was surprised to receive my email many months later asking if she'd agree to be a source of information for my book! I patterned Olivia's aquarium after the one I visited, the Tennessee Aquarium in Chattanooga. However, I tweaked some aspects and obviously located it in North Carolina.

I hope you enjoyed Olivia and Brady's journey. They were both interesting characters to explore and, I'll admit, a bit of a challenge to bring together. Because she's a recent widow, I worked hard to make their love story authentic and believable. If you'd like more information on my suspense or historical books, please visit my website at www.karenkirst.com or visit with me on Facebook. I also like to hear from readers through email, which is karenkirst@live.com.

Blessings,
Karen Kirst

WE HOPE YOU ENJOYED THIS BOOK!

Love Inspired®
SUSPENSE

Uncover the truth in these thrilling
stories of faith in the face of crime
from Love Inspired Suspense.
Discover six new books available
every month, wherever books
are sold!